The Cure Hotel

Ashley S. Clancy

Static House Publishing

Published by Static House Publishing 2016

ISBN: 1539187608

ISBN-13: 978-1539187608

Printed and bound by AM/CS United States

www.goodreads/ashleysclancy.com

Statichouse@btinternet.com

About the Author. Ashley S. Clancy was born in New York and moved to London (England) at the age of six. She studied philosophy before becoming a relationship consultant and running a successful business for almost 30 years. Now semi-retired and after writing an award winning article for a New York magazine in 2008, Clancy plans to embark on a writing career, where "The Cure Hotel" will become her first novel in 2016.

About the book

19 year old Christina Avery has been a receptionist at the Cure Hotel since she was seventeen. During her time at the dark and run down hotel, she has had no fewer than eight sexual encounters with male guests.

This is Christina's journey, as a new manager comes into save the reputation of the horrible hotel, then how one man's vision, is another employees sexual spy hole.

With something sinister and sexual going on in every room and someone always watching those rooms, this highly intense book will keep even the secret voyeur in you holding your breath until the very end.

Contents

CHAPTER 1 – *WELCOME TO THE CURE*

I can't say I have the best job in the world, but it isn't the worst job in the world either. Okay, some might say being a hotel receptionist might not be a real vocation in life, considering I don't intend to move up the ladder in the hotel industry or take my career any further, but the job does have its perks. Fair enough, it's only one perk in particular I'm thinking about right now, but what a perk to have when a hot guy checks in for the night and he's looking to get lucky. And who better to sleep with than me, someone young, attractive and who enjoys sex more than the average type of woman?

Ooh and now thinking about it and looking at myself in my bedroom mirror, here's another perk – The uniform. I mean, in what other job do you get to dress up, wear as much make-up as you like, then get to feel sexy wearing it? Okay, this white blouse might be designed for a slightly older woman than nineteen year old me, but the light blue mini skirt is definitely something I enjoy putting on. I mean, look at my legs – I'm not exactly the tallest person in the world, but I certainly feel taller when there's so much of my legs on show. I must give credit to my former boss, because he did know how to pick a uniform for his staff to wear. Okay, he was a sleaze-ball most of the time and always grabbed at my ass, but at least he made me feel wanted and desirable when I turned up for work. What better way of feeling hot, when your boss talks to you and you can see the outline of his erection all the time? And what's wrong with giving him head a few times, if it stops you getting in trouble for being late?

Which asshole invented sexual harassment in the workplace anyway? I mean, was it my former bosses fault for thinking he'd hired another me, then she turned out to be a scream-rape, happy nun? Fancy arresting and banning him from running a hotel ever again, just for finding one of his employees hot enough to grab at, then her turning him down. Saying that, he shouldn't have tried it on or even hired a police officer's daughter, especially when he had willing me working at the hotel already. That was a fun interview with the police I had that night - Did he ever touch me? No. Did he ever make a move on me? No. Did he ever make a sexual pass at me? No. Lucky for him, I told them nothing. Unfortunate for me, not one person believed me, considering every other female employee said, hell yeah!

The one thing I hate about my job? Dragging myself out of bed at five-thirty in the evening, then working the night shift on reception. Okay, turns out I wouldn't have a job if I didn't, considering our hotel only opens at eight in the evening, but that's beside the point. I mean, when do I get to go out shopping, have my hair done, or dance the night away in a nightclub? If you sleep all day and work all night, you've got to fit the sexy and sex in somewhere, right?

Oh well, that's me ready for another shift. My long blonde hair is brushed to perfection, my uniform is as revealing and as hot as I can make it, and my clean white thong is hopefully going to get really dirty tonight. Let's hope, although I know the hotel I work at is a shit-hole, this new owner coming in to revamp the place, doesn't take my perks away at least. Time to go, or I'm going to be late and I don't think this guy would accept some oral sex to forgive me.

Wow, how standing outside this building never seems to amaze me. Literally a few blocks down the street sits Manhattan and all the wonders it has to offer the world, then hidden out here in a little dark street, this hole! It really must be the dirtiest, broken down looking, disgusting building I've ever seen. I mean – Building, building, house, shop, building, all pleasant enough looking around me. Building, building, shop, shop, then bang - This place. Paint peeling off the brick work, shabby front door spray-canned to the maximum, windows falling out. It really is the worst building in the world and a wonder of the world too, considering I wonder why anyone would ever want to stay here for the night, ever!

Oh well, at least the place has me. Lovely me to brighten up the dampness and make the building warm and sexually damp instead. Here goes nothing – Another shift at the Cure.

"Aah, hello Christina. And early in for your shift too" chirps my new boss, as I walk through the main door.
Would you accept a blow job? Because I wouldn't mind going home, staying in bed for another few hours, then doing this for him instead, if I don't need to be here on time.

This place is a hole and I mean a hole with a huge dark, damp and horrible hole in the middle of it. The reception desk I sit behind looks more like a dirty dinner table - The carpet on the floor, looks as if you blew on it hard enough, it would turn to dust and don't get me started on the... Oh, that was a light switching on for the first time, wasn't it?

"And there you go" sings my boss and the new owner of this hotel, Mr Mike Harper. "One of sixty-three light fixtures to repair in this beautiful building, done" he adds.
I can see the light you've fixed Mr Harper – I can actually see you up that ladder over there – But I don't think your lights are all on, if you think this place is beautiful or ever going to be, just because you've lightened it up. In-fact, I think it would be better them off and broken again, because at least walking into this place right now, you wouldn't be able to see the stale vomit patch over there on the wall, which obviously no-one has ever spotted in the dark before, yet we've all certainly smelled it a few times.

"Okay, that's me done for the day" he chirps, climbing down his ladder, with a huge satisfied smile on his face.

Mike Harper seems to be a really nice man. I mean, he's clearly passionate about this place, but I don't think he's all there. Come on, who would smile knowing they own this hotel? I don't smile that much and I just work here. Still, I give him the credit he deserves - The vision he tells us he has for this place, certainly seems incredible and if he does restore this hole in the way he plans, then I might just be able to walk in here of an evening and not die of embarrassment every time. Unfortunately, one light fixture in an eight hour day, doesn't impress me much and I fear I might be in my sixties before he gets finished.

"Where's Jenna?" I call out, knowing my receptionist colleague and the third and last member of our team is never late.

"She's trying to unlock the basement door" he informs me, closing his ladder and placing it on the floor.

The basement door again? I've been working in this hotel since I was seventeen and that door has never been unlocked.

Speak of the devil, if that devil was an angel sent down from heaven.

"Hi, Christina" chirps my partner, team-mate and sort of friend, Jenna.

As I smile at the female I spend five nights a week with in this place, I can immediately see another day passed hasn't loosened her up any. Jenna wears the same white blouse and blue mini skirt as I do, yet wears it so very differently to me. Whereas my white blouse is open at

5

the top, with a certain amount of cleavage on offer, Jenna's is buttoned up at the neck. In-fact, if there was any more buttons on her blouse at the top, she'd be able to choke herself to death with it. Then of course there's her skirt. My long looking, smooth bare legs make me feel sexy and attractive, whereas she feels better wearing black tights underneath, covering everything up.

"Okay girls, let me give you a quick tour of the place, before I go home to my beautiful wife" sings Mr Harper, showing us that we can see the reception area a lot clearer now the lights are on.

Wow, isn't this place huge? I mean, what a whole lot of empty space, with only a desk in the corner.

"This reception area over the next week or so will be transformed" he explains. "New decoration, flooring and plants are going to brighten it up" he adds, seeming really enthusiastic about this idea.

It's going to take more than a few pot plants to brighten this place up, I'm afraid. Seriously, look at it. I've never seen it in the light, considering I work here when it's dark every evening, but it looks like a prison block - Huge dirty floor space on the ground floor, with four doors leading to rooms, then a huge metal staircase heading up to the four cells on the top floor landing.

"With a clean up, a new reception desk and a modern staircase, this place is going to look fantastic" he continues to sing out.

You had me at fantastic, Mr Harper.

"How many rooms have we got, girls?" he then asks.

"Eight" Jenna and I respond in unison.

"Four on the ground floor and four upstairs" she adds, going one better than me like she always does.

Once Mr Harper has explained that three of the rooms

upstairs have now been renovated and are not to be used until the place is complete, I actually believe he's done more than repair a light fixture today, so instantly open my mouth.

"Can we see one of the finished rooms, right now?" I ask, sounding quite excited.

Fair enough – At this moment in time I'm not thinking about how wonderful the room might look, but a freshening up of the bed sheets really does appeal to me. Seriously, do you know how hard it is to be as sexual as I am, have a nice visitor come to stay, then lay down on the sheets someone else has soiled beforehand? It's really very off putting!

"Once the final room is finished upstairs tomorrow night, I will let you both have a sneak peek, but until then, stay out" he warns us, before declaring all rooms upstairs are now out of service to the public.

Why does him saying we aren't allowed to look, make me feel tonight I'm going to have a look even more so? Oh, where are we heading to now? Okay, he's heading over to the door which isn't a room, but the crap room as we've called it over the years. The room that's been out of service ever since I've worked here and is jam packed full of...

"Wow!" I gasp as he opens the door, all the lights are working in here too.

The other day this room was packed with dusty old furniture and broken pieces of wood, yet today it's empty, clean and nearly as big as the reception area.

"Once I've put a wall up over there, I'm going to build a small kitchen. Then the rest of this space is going to be used as a dining room" he explains.

Do you know what? I can actually vision what he's trying

to do with the place now. Saying that, I still think he should be working on the outside first, considering no visitor is ever going to enter this place if he doesn't.

"Mr Harper, one question" says a confused looking Jenna, pondering on his vision too.

Why does she always look so scared when she wants to ask a question? Ask it already - You'll probably find out it wasn't as confusing or as terrifying as you first thought it was.

"Why do we need a dining area, if we only open our doors at eight in the evening?" she asks.

That's why she looked confused asking it - That's why she's more intelligent than me, because look at my face now, confused as hell by it too, just as interested in the answer myself, yet not ever being a question I would have asked.

Suddenly a huge grin appears on Mr Harper's face, as though he's just won a million dollars or something.

"That's the good news girls" he chirps.

What's the good news, where?

"We're going to turn this place into a hotel that is open twenty-four hours a day" he explains.

Okay Christina, this is your moment - Ask the confusing question in your head, before Jenna beats you to it. You know it's in there, you know you've got one.

"Mr Harper" Jenna chirps at him. "If you only have two staff and we both work at night, how are you going to open during the day?"

Oh crap... That's exactly what I was going to ask, if I knew what I was trying to ask myself.

As the grin on Mr Harper's face grows bigger than I've ever seen it before and boy does this guy like to smile a lot, it's here he confesses his biggest plan of all.

"Jenna you are going to become the day time manageress of the hotel and employ up to three staff to work for you" he explains.

As Jenna's dream and something she constantly nags me about every night becomes a reality, her smile is even bigger than the one on Mr Harper's face right now. Seriously, any wider and they'd be able to swallow the building whole.

"Christina, you will have the same number of employees under you and become my night manageress" he then chirps again.

Sod it – Why couldn't I get the life and have the day time job? Why is he offering her the better... Excuse me? Did you just say manageress? Me? But I'm really just Jenna's sidekick, why would...

Soon enough my grin is wider than their smiles put together and at this moment in time, I wish Mr Harper was my old sleazy boss, so I could thank him sexually, because I'm so excited. As the mini tour of the horrible building continues, I start to feel like I'm the one that's won the million dollar prize.

"In this room, I plan to sound proof the walls and have a bar and a dance floor" he says.

I can't believe this building with the lights on is so much bigger - I can't believe my new boss wants to have a mini nightclub in his hotel - Doesn't he realize I'd live inside a nightclub and go absolutely nuts if...

"I know how much working of a night destroys your social life Christina, so when the hotel is full and is on lock down in the future, I expect you to be in here entertaining the guests and having lots of fun" he explains.

Wow, maybe he does know me after all.

Although the hotel is a long way from turning into a classy establishment and he seems to be doing all the work himself on a budget, I am really excited about this. I mean, yesterday I just turned up to receive a wage, but tonight I could quite happily clean those vomit stains off the wall with my bare hands to help out. This is amazing and with one closed door in front of us to be shown, I can't wait to find out what he has planned for this space too.

"That's it girls, my vision" he says.

Come on then Jenna, question the last door. You know you want to be the first to say it. No? Okay then, I will...

"What about that door over there, Mr Harper?" I ask, realizing Jenna is asking nothing about it.

"That's the door leading to the secret passage way behind the rooms, Christina. There's one upstairs too. They have all the electrics and wires inside" responds Jenna, obviously showing me why she didn't ask and why she knows so much more than I do about this hotel.

"Right, I've really got to get home to the wife, so you two have a great night and thanks for all your hard work so far" Mr Harper says, picking up his jacket.

As Jenna takes all the news in her stride, because she always wanted to become the manageress, I wave him off at the desk, still beaming from ear to ear.

"Oh and I have some wonderful new uniforms turning up in the next few days, so we can class this place up a little more" he calls back, looking me up and down, then at my legs before saying it.

On a normal day I'd instantly take offense to this kind of comment, but yeah, let's do it – Let's class up the place.

I'd be happy wearing a penguin outfit right now!

Two minutes before our shift officially starts, Jenna walks over to the main door and declares the place open like she usually does. Meanwhile, I take a long lingering look around the tattered old building and still vision the classy establishment this hotel is going to become. Obviously, I'm going to do my best as manageress – Obviously, I'm going to do my best by our guests – And obviously, with a classier hotel comes classier male visitors, which should mean a better quality of orgasm for me when I have sex with one of them. Hey, you can take the sex out of a building and class it up, but you can't take it out of me!

Jenna and I work really well together and although we are like chalk and cheese, we seem to cater for each-others needs. For some reason, although Jenna is completely professional in every sense of the word, she isn't that great at time keeping. Don't get me wrong, she's never late for work, but when on a break half way through the night, she can sometimes return up to two hours later. This bothered me when she first started working here, because I thought she was sleeping somewhere whilst I struggled to stay awake, but since she caught me having sex with a random guest behind the reception desk six months ago, we seem to have an unspoken agreement in place, where she has my back and I have hers, no questions asked. Yes Jenna is well educated – Yes she knows a lot more about the running of a hotel than I do; with her degree in hotel management behind her, but she's down to earth and that's good enough to make this work. Yes she speaks proper all the time – Yes she talks to the guests a little anally sometimes and yes I think she's a virgin, but I don't judge. Saying that, she can't be a virgin, because she's always banging on about her perfect fiance Greg, unless of course he's a virgin too, or a fictional character. Fancy getting engaged so young? I mean, I'm nineteen just like her, but you wouldn't see me settling for just one guy any time soon. I think that's mental – I think that's a waste – Still, as I said, I don't judge, so good luck to her.

$9:02$pm (Monday 22nd March)

Well, that's an hour into our shift tonight and not one person has come through the front door. Considering we've only got four rooms on offer right now that could actually be a blessing, but you'd think someone would need a bed for the night? Jenna's off around the hotel, doing whatever it is that she does and I'm just sitting here at this horrible desk, scraping nasty bits of chewing gum off the underneath, in my bid to help this place move into the future. Not that I wasn't the one that stuck the chewing gum here in the first place of course – Maybe it was me, maybe it wasn't, who cares, but this really is the boring part of the... Oh look, we have a visitor at last.

"Evening Darling, room number one again please, if you don't mind"

This is sure of himself, Gary Sheen. He comes here up to three times a week, checks in with a different prostitute every time, then leaves after a few hours. I'm sure there are much nicer hotels out there to be having sex in, but Gary is so up himself, I don't suppose the crusty sheets he left behind after his last visit bothers him much. Yes I know, this sounds disgusting, but what do you expect in a place like this, fresh towels and a change of bed sheets every day? We have no washing machine, no laundry service and the best our former owner did was replace the dirty sheets once a month with cheap new ones. When I'm manageress of this place, one of my three employees will be a maid to keep everything fresh and clean. One, because it's nice and two, because I'd never clean someone's warm, sweaty sheets for them myself.

"Room one is available tonight, Mr Sheen. Are you staying alone, or paying for another guest too?" I ask, in my poshest receptionist voice, noticing a tart hasn't followed him in yet like I'm expecting.

"Even if I wasn't alone, you know I'd still be paying for two people, don't you Christina?" he chirps in my direction. "You know Gary Sheen never leaves here without getting laid" he adds as sure of himself, like he was just a few days ago.

"So, that's a room for two then?" I question confirming his booking, before processing it.

"As always, two people" he answers.

"And will she be checking in with you, or at a later time?" I ask, knowing we have this same conversation every time.

"Later, Christina" he answers, with a cocky smile, claiming he always wants to give me first refusal.
Every time without fail, the same lines are delivered.

"I will tell you, like I tell you, every other day Mr Sheen. We had sex about a year ago and I won't be doing it ever again" I respond, with a huge friendly smile on my face, but making my point yet again.

"Oh why? Why not Christina, why? I was a good lover, wasn't I?" he questions, doing his predictable sulking routine.

"As I always tell you Mr Sheen, you were incredible that night, but I don't want to do it again" I respond, claiming I'm a good girl.

Once he's done his why question again, like always I tell him exactly why I won't sleep with him again.

"You pay prostitutes for sex every few nights, Mr Sheen. Five hundred dollars a time. You left me a five dollar tip that night"

"But I didn't think you'd appreciate me paying you like a hooker. I thought I was doing the right thing" he laughs, like he usually does at this stage of the conversation.

"That's you checked in Mr Sheen" I playfully sigh at him, knowing we will have this exact same conversation in two or three days time, just as his latest prostitute friend walks into the building.

Now, shall I crouch down to pick up and hand over his key-card tonight, or shall I... Sod it, let's bend over, I'm in a really good mood, considering I will become manageress and enjoy banning him from this hotel very soon.

As I bend, my short skirt rides up, and as he watches my white thong appear before his eyes, I know it's coming. It's the reach over the desk, grab my left buttock cheek and squeeze routine. And there is it.

"As I always tell you Mr Sheen, you can touch, but you cannot have" I whisper, as his date joins him at the other side of the desk and he gives me a wink.

Once I've handed over his key-card, I watch as the long legged prostitute follows him towards his room, something down below tells me I should have taken him up on his offer like it always does, but these days I always seem to want to wait, just in-case someone better walks through the front door.

9:42pm (Monday 22ⁿᵈ March)

"Has Gary shown up tonight? I just heard noises coming from room number one, as I came past?" asks Jenna, turning up from wherever she's been hiding.
Once I've confirmed Mr Sheen has checked in and predictably will be checking out before midnight again, Jenna and I sit down at the desk together, where I know what happens next. This is the time where she loves to tell me how wonderful her life is and how after every shift ends at eight in the morning, she goes home and has the world's best sex with this Greg guy. I mean, if her stories weren't so desperate sounding all the time, I would actually stop believing she's a virgin.

"I got home at eight thirty this morning and was absolutely exhausted" she starts telling me, as I try not to rudely yawn. "There was Greg lying on the rose petal covered bed completely naked" she adds.
See what I mean? Who does this? Why does every story about this Greg guy need to sound so perfectly romantic? Why can't she just come in and tell me he ravished her anally or something? Why do I believe it's all made up and she's still a virgin? Because it really sounds like she goes home, picks up a romantic novel and reads the thing until she believes it's her in the book. Don't get me wrong, I love Jenna, but I wish she would just skip to the good bits quicker. Oh that's right, there are never any good bits are there, only perfect bits...

"So, as I was saying. I got home and there they were. Five different colors of rose petals scattered all over the bed"

See, even if this was true and he was this soft, surely red one's alone would have sufficed? Who needs five colors? Are there even five different colors of rose petals? I mean, it's as though...

"Hold that thought Jenna" I chirp, noticing someone else walking into the hotel.

"Oh god, it's Bill" she whispers, as I hear the disgust in her voice, without looking at the disapproval on her face, although I know it's etched right beside me.

"Good evening Mr Hodge. Room for one tonight, is it?" I ask, leaping straight back into my receptionist voice, always knowing with Bill, it's a room for one.

Bill has been coming to this hotel for years. He's quiet, he's harmless and he's polite. He's also creepy, always freakishly dressed, and if he pulled a knife out and offered to stab someone to death, you wouldn't be surprised.

"Y... y... yes, r... r... room for one" he responds in his usually scary stutter, as he ticks, shakes and tries desperately to control it.

Every single time this guy speaks to me, it sends a shiver of dread up my spine!

Once again, he's harmless, so I hand him his key-card as quickly as possible, before he can stare us both to death.

There he goes, he's on his merry way, dragging his feet towards his room, walking like the living dead. Remember what I said about forty year old Gary Sheen's crusty sheets and changing them? I'd rather hand wash them myself, than enter fifty year old Bill's room when he's staying. Wow, he's creepy! The creepiest thing about Bill? When a visitor pays to stay at a hotel, they are free to roam as they please, right? Bill never stays in his room. Where this huge reception area is empty and only has our desk sitting out here, Bill will often pull a chair out of his room, sit himself down in a corner and watch us work all night. Seriously, it's probably one of the most harmless things to take place during the night, but something that's often made me have nightmares. It's as though he watches us, weighing up his prey and although he's never actually done anything, Jenna and I both feel it's only a matter of time before he strikes. Obviously, Bill is another guest I will ban from visiting when I become...

"C... C... Chris... Christina, Jenna" he then calls out as he opens his room door.

Thank god he said her name too.

"Con... c... con... congratulations on y... y... your promotion" he stutters.

We would ask how he knows this, but considering that would mean us talking to him, we both smile, wave and wish him a pleasant night.

As Bill disappears into his room to do god-knows what, it's as though an instant weight is always lifted from around our shoulders, as we always sigh together, then sit down again. It's in-fact at times like this when I wished I dressed more like Jenna, because I do happen to feel slightly more violated by Bill's stare than Jenna seemingly does.

"So, as I was saying. Five different colors of rose petals scattered all over the bed" Jenna begins to sing out once more.

17

Holy shit... Do you really feel like talking romance at me again, after welcoming Bill into the building?

10:28pm (Monday 22ⁿᵈ March)

With two out of the four available rooms checked into, we both realize that we'll be lucky to have another guest stay with us tonight. Then once Jenna has bored me to death about her whole yesterday morning sex thing with Greg, knowing I'm going to listen to a different version of her romance novel tomorrow night too, it's about now that she does her disappearing act. Hold on... Someone else is walking in. Gary Sheen is already here. Bill Hodge is in the building too. We never usually have more than these two guys staying. Wow, who are you guys?

"Welcome to the Cure hotel, how may I help you?" sings Jenna beside me.

Now that's how it's done professionally. Why do I get to check in our seedy regulars, yet Jenna always jumps on board when fresh faces appear in front of our desk?

"We've been all over Manhattan and can't find anywhere else to stay" explains a man, standing beside a woman, who I assume is his wife.

Shame, because if he was alone, I would definitely of...

"We have two more rooms available at a fee of two hundred dollars per night" sings Jenna in her posh voice.

What the...? We only charge Bill and Gary twenty dollars a night and that's only when we have the courage to charge them for our disgusting service at all - So how is this possible?

"Oh, you're such a life saver" responds the man, pulling out his credit card to pay, with a huge relieved looking smile on his face.

I guess that's why Jenna is more suitable to this management job than I am then. I would have paid them to stay here tonight!

10:52pm (Monday 22nd March)

I have no idea where Jenna has disappeared to, but I still can't get over the fact she took two hundred dollars from that poor couple for the night. Two hundred dollars? I mean, I don't think we made that much over the whole of last month! Oh well, the hotel is almost at full capacity, I can't see anyone else out there desperate enough to stay here tonight and it's nearly eleven o'clock. Eleven o'clock, which only means one thing - Jenna's disappeared so she doesn't have to do the horrible coke run.

The minute I think it, the second I fear it, it happens - The phone rings. I know nobody ever rings our hotel, I know Mr Harper doesn't call during the night, which only leaves one person.

"Hello, the Cure Hotel, Christina speaking, how can I help you?" I sing down the phone, already knowing who it is at the other end.

"C... c... can I ha... ha... have a cold c... c... coke delivered to m... m... m... my room?"

Mr Bill Hodge – Always at around eleven o'clock - Always when Jenna disappears - And always my worst nightmare on any shift.

I remember my first week working here, long before Jenna started and I worked with a bitch called Mandy. I remember getting my first ever room service call, then taking that drink to Mr Hodge's room. I remember him telling me to come in and I remember the vision that left me scarred for life. Him, sitting on his bed watching porn – Him, sitting in his dirty stained Y-fronts – Him, telling me to take a seat on his bed next to him. Oh how I almost quit my job that night and oh how I've never fallen for it since!

As I knock at Mr Hodge's door, knowing what's going to come next, I brace myself for impact, although I've now done this a million times over.

"C... come in" he calls, from inside the room.
And there goes the cold shiver up my spine - There goes my legs.

"Coming in" I call, as though he needs any warning, whilst opening his door with my key-card pass. "It's inside your room, at the door, Mr Hodge" I then call out like I always do, placing his drink on the floor and closing the door behind me.
That has got to be the biggest sigh of relief I take at work every single night and although Jenna does do the coke run from time to time, she often disappears at this time.

"Have you done your coke run then?" whispers Gary Sheen, suddenly emerging from his room.
I always try to remain professional looking and not affected by this traumatic event, but Gary has been around long enough to know what goes on.

"Disgusting pervert trying to get you into his room again?" he asks, finding it more amusing that I do.
Once again, I try to play it down and refuse to admit to another guest that someone else is perverted, but it's too hard to cover up.
Suddenly because stupid Gary has kept me talking, Bill then opens his door behind me.

"Oh e... e... excuse me C... C... Christina. Just going f... f... for a walk" he says, chair in hand.

Great and before I've had the chance to compose myself again, he's now going to sit in the corner of reception and watch me. Shit... Who lightened up this reception area? I'm going to be able to see him watching me all night, instead of uncomfortably feeling it, aren't I?

As I let weird Bill take his chair to wherever he plans to sit tonight, I walk back over to the desk with Gary to check him out of the hotel.

"Where is she then?" I ask, making him aware that I can't check him out, whilst his partner for the night is still in the room.

Although I know I can and he does too, I deliberately stall proceedings until Bill out of the corner of my eye has settled and sat down.

"How do you put up with it?" Gary whispers, from the other side of the desk.

"Put up with what?" I ask, knowing exactly what he's talking about, but reverting back to my professional manner.

"The old weird guy watching you like he does?" he asks.

Suddenly I feel the urge to be sarcastic, knowing Mr Sheen is about to leave anyway.

"Him over there in the corner? You checking me out close up? What's the difference?" I respond, feeling the need to defend Bill slightly, whilst calling Mr Sheen a pervert playfully too.

With that his lady-friend emerges from the room and Gary is on his way.

"Maybe next time, Christina" he whispers, heading

21

towards the main door.

In your dreams, I think to myself, as my smile gives him this sign too.

"W... w... why do y... y... you let him t... t... treat you that w... way?" calls Bill from his corner.

Fucking hell Jenna, where are you? Please don't leave me alone out here with freaky Mr Hodge.

"Like what, Mr Hodge?" I call back, standing firmly behind the desk, making out I've got paperwork to do.

"He, he... he talks to y... you like, like you're a... s... s... slag?"

Okay Christina, pretend he didn't just say that. Smile, nod, do anything except engage in conversation with him.

"I... I... I know... know you... you slept with him once" he continues to stutter.

First he knows about our promotion and now he knows about this, yet how? What does he do, hold a glass up to the.... Damn it, don't think it – It will only creep you out and give you nightmares.

"It... it's o... o... okay C... Christina. I'm not, not, not h... hurt that you had s... s... sex with him"

Okay, I'm officially freaking out now!

"Just... Just d... Don't let him use y... you"

"Okay Mr Hodge, I won't. If you will excuse me for one moment, I need to find Jenna quickly" I call out, deciding to end the horribly uncomfortable conversation and quickly leave my post.

"I... I.... I know w... where she..."

"Don't worry yourself Mr Hodge, I will find her" I call back, not surprised he thinks he knows where she is already, considering he probably does, but needing to escape more.

11:36pm (Monday 22nd March)

I didn't find Jenna earlier, not that I actually looked for her. What I did instead was strange really, because whereas I normally get freaked out by Bill watching us for a few hours, I decided to hide out of the way and watch him instead. Obviously I was waiting for him to go back into his room, but whilst watching him, I couldn't help but wonder, why does he come here most nights? Why does he watch us like that? I mean, it's not like he's ever said anything from his darkened corner, now lit up. Is he just a lonely old man? What would a man his age actually do if a nineteen year like me made a move on him? Not that I ever would, but there's got to be some reasoning behind it all, surely?

Once I watched Bill stagger back to his room with his chair; giving up on me at last, I quickly appear from my shadowed corner on the second floor. Strangely, Jenna appears at exactly the same time, as though she's been watching too.

"Have you been watching or something?" I joke with her, knowing I've been doing the same.

"What's wrong with you Christina? Of course I haven't been watching. What are you calling me? What are you trying to say?" she starts randomly yelling at me.

Okay, she's either been hiding away talking on the phone to her beloved Greg and had a bust-up, or she's just got her period. Either way, I never meant anything by it, you touchy bitch!

23

1:02 am (Tuesday 23rd March)

Usually at this time of the morning, I take my break and Jenna has already had her hour at twelve. Normally I can't wait to get out of his place for an hour, but considering Miss Grumpy-Knickers hasn't said a word to me for the last hour, I'm ready to run tonight!

My break usually sees me do this walk, where I leave the hotel, wander across the street, to enter the only bar in this part of town. Okay, this might not be the area a young girl should be strutting her stuff in a mini skirt at this hour of the morning, but considering everyone knows me around here, I think I'm safe enough. Besides, if anyone is going to be attacked, I think all the guys around here know it will be me making the moves, not them!

"Morning Christina, Usual?" calls friendly barman Dean, as I walk into the place.

See? Everyone knows me around here.

"Had sex with any guests tonight?" he then asks, talking to me as though I'm one of the lads.

Talking of lads, this place is also where I come if the talent is poor over at the hotel. There's always a good ten or so men in here and not much in the way of female competition either. Unfortunately on some nights like it is tonight, poor pickings at the hotel sometimes means poor pickings here as well.

This is usually the hour where I enjoy my sixty minutes of freedom, recapture my missed nights out, then cram a night full of fun into one single hour. Okay, so in the past I've taken two or three hours on occasions but as I said,

Jenna and I don't question each-other, so it works.

"What's going on in here tonight, Dean? Where is everyone?" I ask, approaching the bar, as my drink is served.

"A new bar has just opened in the next town, so that's where everyone is" he explains.

Wow, I wonder how my tiny club across the road is going to impact his business when it opens?

"Are you in one of those sexy moods tonight, Christina?" he asks.

"I might be" I flirt, quickly realizing he's talking sex, as though he talks anything else, whilst I down my drink.

"Well, you know you've always got me to fall back on" he chuckles, ready to offer me another drink.

Dean's a nice guy. I think he's around twenty-five and yes I've had sex with him a few times in the last year. Thing is, he doesn't know this, but he's too easy. I like a bit of a challenge, not somebody who's there for the picking every time. Fact is, I could snap my fingers and have Dean whenever I like, but it's not the same. I want to be with a man, where I think about not having him, then wanting him more before I've even started. Dean is whatever I want him to be and that's not a turn on.

"Maybe tomorrow night, Sexy" I tell him. "Jenna's got her knickers in a twist about something over at the hotel, so I'd better go and sort it out" I add, blowing him a kiss as I leave.

Once I do return to the hotel after having a drink at the bar, the rest of the night really drags. It's even worse when Jenna's got the hump and doesn't want to talk about anything. Seriously, if I thought it was possible for us to talk right now, I'd ask her about those bloody rose petals again.

From 2am to seven in the morning, it's always a long hard slog. Girlie magazines are literally dissected and toes are painted so many times, it's a wonder I can get my shoes on the next day. All the guests are asleep, the place becomes eerily quiet and all we can do is force our eyes to stay open until Mr Harper shows up. Luckily for me with the vision of becoming manageress and the little nightclub about to be built, I'm still living the dream, dreaming about it all with my eyes half open.

$7:55$am (Tuesday 23rd March)

"Good morning girls, how was your night?" sings Mr Harper, walking into the building.
This is the part of the day that really confuses me the most. I mean, he's been home to bed, yet walks in here as fresh as anything, yet shouldn't we be more awake than him, considering we haven't been to bed yet? Either way, Jenna and I greet him like we do every morning, with a yawn, a stretch and a one word answer, before he asks us who he's checking out this morning after we've gone home.

"There's a couple in room three and Bill Hodge is in room two" says Jenna.

"Is that all we had stay here last night?" he asks, looking a little disappointed.

"Gary Sheen stayed too, but he had to check out early" Jenna tells him.

"Why does he always do that? Why have I never met this guy?" he asks.

Neither Jenna nor I are going to tell him what goes on behind closed hotel doors, are we? Besides, it's not like we can prove it anyway, because we've never actually seen it for ourselves. Well, I've experienced it for myself, but never caught him in the act with a prostitute.

"Oh well girls, get yourselves home to bed" Mr Harper sings, promising the final room upstairs will be finished later on today and we will get to have a look.

CHAPTER 2 – *ANOTHER NIGHT*

Do I feel like getting out of bed today? Do I heck! To be perfectly honest, I could stay here in bed, close my eyes and sleep for another three or four hours at least. I can't work out if I haven't slept enough during the day, or if when I got home this morning, I couldn't get to sleep straight away. Obviously I know I didn't sleep, because I couldn't stop thinking about my new role at the hotel, but surely I've slept at little?

Okay Christina, get yourself out of bed, then like a zombie head through into the bathroom and have a shower. That's right, the bathroom is to the left of your bedroom door, not half asleep swaying towards the right. Come on, now is definitely not the time to start turning up late, so wake up and get with it. I can't help but feel I... Was that the front door? Surely not.

Look at this – I'm so tired, so dead on my feet, that I even have to make sure I'm wearing my pajamas before heading to the front door.

"Okay, I'm coming. I'm coming" I grumble, not feeling awake enough to call out, as I stumble towards the door. Who could this possibly be? No-one ever visits me at half five in the evening – Everyone knows at this time I'm getting up and ready for work.

As I reach out to open the door, I can't work out if I'm sleep walking or more miffed that someone keeps knocking so rudely, I slowly open the door deciding to find out who it is first, before kicking off and... Oh no, this can't be right – This isn't good.

"M... m... Mr Hodge. What are you doing here?" I nervously stutter in shock, instantly worried that he might think I'm mocking his real stutter.

"Y... you hid away l... l... last night and... and... and didn't let m... m... me watch you" he responds.
Okay, so I guess this is all it takes to wake me up fully, but what's he going on about?

"I'm sorry Mr Hodge, but I don't know what you're talking about" I quickly tell him, feeling I need to be professional, although this intrusive visit somehow tells me I've got a right to be upset. "How about we talk about this when I get to work?" I suggest.

"No!" he answers abruptly.
Okay, what's freakier? A one word, shut down answer from him, or an answer without a creepy stutter? The answer? Me standing on my doorstep, keeping the door ajar by force, wearing my pajamas, that's what!

"Look Mr Hodge, I need to get ready for work, so if you don't mind" I adamantly say deciding that's enough, rudely attempting to close the door on him.

"No!" he answers abruptly again, this time forcing his foot into my doorway, preventing it from closing.

Okay, this is now turning into something from a horror movie and I don't like it.

"Mr Hodge, move your foot, or I will be forced to call the police and have you banned from our hotel" I grunt, giving him every chance to do the right thing.

I ease off the door slightly, simply to let him take his foot away.

"No!" he then growls, forcing the door in on me, as I stagger back through my hallway off balance.

Intrusion, turned horror movie, turned the real scary deal. Okay, why is he coming in? Why is he now closing the door behind him? Why is he looking at me like that?

"Mr Hodge, you can't enter someone's apartment like this, it's not right" I tell him, steadying myself against the wall. "What do you want?" I ask, backing down my hallway slightly, as he creepily staggers towards me.

"Y... y... you have sex with m... m... men at... at the hotel" he stutters. "Now, it... it... it's m... m... my turn" he adds, making his intentions clear.

"Okay Mr Hodge, no problem. Let's have sex at the hotel tonight then" I chirp out, trying to force myself to sound enthusiastic about it. "You go there now and I will meet you there in about an hour" I tell him, feeling it's not exactly convincing, but it's worth a try.

"NO!" he yells out. "Sex w... with me n... n... now or die" he adds.

Okay, I've had enough of this. I don't care about my job, because seriously, no job is worth this. Now, shall I overpower him? Kick him in the balls? Or just punch him in the face for doing this to me? Either way, I'd better make a decision quickly, because I'm running out of hallway and I don't fancy leading him into my bedroom behind me and...

"OUCH!" I scream, feeling the full force of his strike.

Oh no, what's happening now? Why is he on top of me? Why am I now on my bed? Oh my god, I must have passed out when he hit me. Oh please, please, please tell me he isn't on top of me, doing things? Oh my god, I feel sick, I... I don't know what to... Okay scream Christina, scream now!

Do I want to get out of bed today? Fuck yeah I do! Why do I keep having these horrible nightmares about Mr Hodge? Seriously, I don't know what's worse - Having this happen for real, or me continuing to have these horrible dreams over and over again? Okay Christina, shake it off. It didn't happen, it never happened.

I head into the bathroom, trying to blank it out, stripping off to have my shower. My god, that felt so real, yet I don't even wear pajamas to bed, so why would I believe it in a dream? Come on Christina, don't stand here under the shower, trying to wash it out of your mind, whilst stupidly still thinking about it – Think about something else. MM-mm yeah, that's right, something else. Let's wash myself and think about me having sex. Oh dear, how can I think sex after the dream I've just had? How? Because that wasn't real and your thoughts about sex right now, are. Why am I so routine when it comes to my sex life? A day after sex, I'm fine to go without it – Two days after it, I start wanting it again – Then by day three

I'm gagging for it like a nymphomaniac? This is in-fact day two, so I'd better get myself some action today, or I'm going to head into day three, where I simply turn into the girl who would and often does sleep with anyone. In-fact, maybe this is day three already. I mean, who is actually counting? When was the last time I had a man? Wow, it's been quite a while really, hasn't it? Fair enough I masturbated a couple of days ago, but that wasn't really sex, was it? Okay, decision made, I need a man today!

On a mission to get to work on time and find a man to have sex with tonight, I get out of the shower and reach for my trusty uniform, where tonight I'm probably going to want the thing ripped off me, like it's been ripped off, manhandled and sometimes torn off in the past. God, I love sex – Wow, how I adore having an orgasm – Oh how I'm so pleased this level of thinking and that shower has helped me to stop thinking about that horrible dream I had this morning. Although now thinking this, it's bloody back again, isn't it?

"Shit..."

7:43pm (Tuesday 23rd March)

Wow, I'm early for work again – This is starting to become a good habit, if that habit was once bad, which it was. Oh dear, looks like Mr Harper hasn't done any work on the outside of the building again today. Maybe I should tell him how I feel or my thoughts? After all, isn't that what a future manageress would do when she spots a problem? No, surely telling him the outside of his building is shocking, would sound patronizing? I mean, it's not like he doesn't walk past it himself every single day. Of course he knows we're not going to attract new guests until the outside is done. Yeah, he will definitely...

"So, it's just a thought Mr Harper..." I then hear, as Jenna walks our manager out into the street, clearly to show him something.

"Oh hello Christina. How's my new night manageress this evening? It's good to see you turning up early for work once again" Mr Harper greets me, rudely cutting Jenna off, although it would have been ruder for him to ignore me, I think.

Yeah definitely ruder, considering Jenna hasn't said hello to me yet and now she looks upset, because I interrupted her, even though I didn't, did I?

"Christina, come over here. Jenna's got an idea" calls Mr Harper.

Stop talking to me Mr Harper. Don't you realize I've got to put up with her all night long? Jenna in a good mood? Nice evening. Jenna in a bad mood? Long night. Saying that... Jenna in bad mood? Doesn't speak to me much. Jenna in a good mood? Another boring fictional love story about her and Greg. Wow, I think even one of her romantic tales right now would get me going, because I'm feeling so horny. Wow, hasn't Mr Harper got a cute little....

"Sorry Mr Harper, what was that?" I then force myself to say, realizing I haven't heard a word he or Jenna have just said standing here outside the hotel.

"Jenna thinks I should work a little on the outside of the hotel rather than the inside, in a bid to attract more visitors" he says, asking me what I think.

I think that's what I've been thinking since yesterday and I'm now angry at myself for not saying it sooner.

"Yeah, Jenna does have a good point" I answer, forcing

a smile onto my face.

Hey, at least me agreeing with her idea has put a smile back on her face.

As we're all in agreement that the boss should do a little touching up outside during the day tomorrow, we head inside to find out what he's worked on today. Instantly I'm hit in the face by just how clean the reception area is. Okay, the horrible desk is still over in the corner and nothing else has been added furniture wise, but the floor is sparkling and the vomit stain on the wall has now gone. It smells fresher in here, the lights are now helping the floor shine and yeah, he's done a good job.

"Okay girls, follow me" he then sings out, walking over to the door beside room number four.

Wow, look at that. He's put a little sign on the door, with the words (*Dining room*) on it. MM-mm, I wonder if he's... No, there's no sign on my little nightclub door yet. Come on then, let's see what you've done in here then. Polished all the floors, if I'm guessing right and...

"Wow!" I gasp, just like I did at this room yesterday.

Two days ago this room was full of junk. Yesterday it was cleared. Now it seems the tables and chairs have been laid out and a huge wall over in the corner shows where the kitchen is going to go. There's no doubt about it, this guy works really hard during the day, whilst Jenna and I sleep at home, but there's only one thing I want to see – A finished room.

"Come on then, let me show you one of the finished rooms upstairs" he chirps, walking us out of the dining room, towards the metal prison style staircase, assuring us this too is being replaced tomorrow.

As the metal under out feet on the old staircase echo's

out around the half empty building; seemingly getting bigger by the day, we reach the top floor where this narrow corridor is sparkling too. As he puts his key-card to room number eight, I really don't know what to expect, then still don't once the door is opened.

Speechless seems to be the only thing coming to mind, considering nothing is coming out of my mouth.

"Well, what do you both think of our new style of room?" he asks.

"It... It... It looks like a real hotel room" I stutter, terrorized by the sheer beauty.

Hey, at least I said something. Plain Jane-Jenna is standing right beside me, sobbing for some reason.

Let me make sense of this in my head. Downstairs in rooms 1 to 4, they are disgusting. I'm talking nasty 70s style peeling wallpaper on the walls, not to mention the damp patches everywhere. The beds are falling apart, the sheets and curtains are dirty and don't get me started on the en-suite, because we should have a danger sign on those doors. Up here however in rooms 5 to 8, I said it correctly the first time – It looks like a hotel. It's fresh, the walls are perfectly painted white. Yes one or two things need finishing off, but the new bed looks incredible. MM-mm, why am I feeling I want to be the first person to christen them all?

"Girls, I can't do the silent treatment any longer. What do you think?" Mr Harper asks again, realizing we're still standing in the doorway, jaws ajar, unlike the door that is proudly wide open.

As we enter the new room it's even better close up, because at every turn, something else appears before my eyes. Look at that, he's even replaced the huge 80s style TV set and gone all flat screen in here.

"What is that hole in the wall over there?" I then question pointing over to it, because in my head it can only be described as a glory hole, but I don't want to say it like this.

"That's where I'm going to put the new automatic control pad. A control pad that controls everything in the room" he boasts. "Soon enough the curtains, the TV and the lighting will all be controlled by a single touch" he adds.

I'm thinking we can charge a little more than the twenty dollars we currently charge, based on this room. Saying that, a sense of over-protectiveness has just come over me and I certainly don't want horrible visitors using these rooms any longer, even if that does mean I stop having sex with them. Yeah, I can masturbate alone on these beds, so no need for dirty old men!

"Once I've finished the downstairs rooms, the dining room, the mini nightclub and the outside, we will be able to open this hotel properly" he explains with pride, before announcing he's done in and needs to go home.

And so he should feel proud, doing all this alone and getting to this stage already.

"Okay girls, just one more surprise before I go" he says, walking us back down the staircase, warning us again the rooms upstairs aren't permitted to be used until it's all finished.

Look at this, he's walking us over to the nightclub door. Surely he hasn't finished this room already too? No he hasn't I think to myself, as he opens the door... But there is a lot of plastic in here.

"This is the new furniture for the reception area" he

tells us. "A new twelve piece seating area, plants over in the corner, and under this sheet, a new reception desk" he shows us, claiming we're the ones who are going to be busy setting it all up tonight.

Although I love the inclusion into your plans Mr Harper, I fear or rather predict, I ain't going to get much of a say with Jenna around tonight. I guess that if it's left down to her, I will be checking in the guests and she will be doing all this exciting stuff. Just a guess, but...

"Jenna, I want you to take care of the desk and set it up with the new computer. Christina, I want you to set up the seating area" he says, heading for the main door, on his way out.

Are you hearing this? It's as though he can read my mind, because it's as though he's said this because he understands Jenna can be a bossy cow sometimes.

"Once you've taken care of your own jobs, you can put your heads together and sort out where the plants are going to go"

As long as I get the seating area, I think I will let Jenna have the plants too. I mean, that will give me time to find a spot to satisfy my sexual urge tonight, won't it? Maybe in one of those new rooms, when Jenna isn't looking. No Christina– Bad Christina... Professional, well behaved and hard working is what you're going to be from now on, not slutty.

8:21pm (Tuesday 23ʳᵈ March)

"Wow, Bill's in early this evening" Jenna whispers, as we stand at the door with all the new furniture inside, then notice him coming in.

"Check him in or do the coke run later?" I whisper

quickly, wanting to give Jenna the choice, considering I will be doing both if it's left down to her.

"I will check him in" she quickly answers, with a smiling frown.

Although I knew she'd never pick the coke run; because it freaks her out more than it does me, I'm pleased she's willing to do something at least, which shows I'm sometimes a little too quick to judge her.

As I watch Jenna walk over to our old desk; which will be gone after tonight, I take to entering this room beside me, then start ripping the plastic off all my new seats, feeling like a happy kid at Christmas.

"Watch that p... p... plastic C... C... Christina. Plastic can be very d... dang... dangerous" calls Bill Hodge from the desk, watching me through the door I stupidly left open.

Should I kick the door shut? Should I smile and humor him? Why the hell has this cold shiver shot up my spine again? Oh great... And now I've just remembered that horrible dream I had about him today. MM-mm, there's an idea...

Once I've done my polite welcome to the Cure tonight at Mr Hodge, I have an idea. The idea is simple – Make some new rules that will make my job here of a night at little easier. Now by rights I should talk these ideas over with Jenna first, but what the hell, she will agree anyway.

As I run over to the desk where they're both standing, I grab a piece of paper and a pen, then head off again. Then I notice Jenna watching me with suspicious eyes, as I take a huge potted plant and race it through reception like a crazy woman.

"Okay, what are you up to Christina?" Jenna asks, walking over to me, as creepy Mr Hodge staggers towards his usual hole for the night.

I quickly explain my plan and tell her the piece of paper is to hang on Mr Hodge's door, claiming new seating is available in reception, so there's no need to carry a chair out of a room. I then explain that his usual spot in the corner, isn't going to be somewhere he watches us from any longer, because I've placed a huge tree in the way.

"Once I've set up the seating area right in front of our new desk, it's going to be very open and lit up" I finally tell her, claiming he isn't going to like sitting right in front of us with the lights shining in his tormented eyes.

With that Jenna is on-board and races over to the room where the new desk sits, then starts unwrapping it, like a kid at Christmas too.

8.55pm (Tuesday 23rd March)

We actually finished designing the new reception area so fast, that we didn't have time to take it all in ourselves. The old desk almost fell apart as we carried it through into the nightclub room to await Mr Harper in the morning, and the new chrome desk is finally set in place, making this area of the hotel look amazing. The plants add character and warmth, whilst the seats I've placed in front of our desk are chrome and leather, looking like a proper grown-up waiting room.

"Wow, look at this place!" sings Gary Sheen, arriving to instantly attempt to lower our new high standard already. "Am I in the right hotel?" he jokes, heading towards us at our new desk.

"Have you forgotten you entertained a lady friend

40

only yesterday Mr Sheen? You don't normally do two days in a row" I respond, not exactly being the professional I should be, but excited by our new look so much, that his seedy nights are no longer welcome here.

"Room for two, is it Mr Sheen?" asks Jenna, ready to boot up our new computer system.

"Yeah, unless you two lovelies would like to join me and my lady friend when she arrives. Which would then become a room for four and a pleasurable night for the both of you" he answers, in his usual cock-sure tone.

I've got to give credit to Gary Sheen, because he just doesn't know when to quit. Oh how I've loved entertaining you over the last few years, Gary - Oh how I love smiling and humoring you right now - But oh how I can't wait to stop you entering this building when we finally open for real.

"So, what's going on girls? Does this new guy in charge really think he's going to add some class to this shit-hole?" he asks, as Jenna does her magic on the new computer screen beside me.

As I feel slightly offended by his comment and Jenna in a more professional mood takes control of the situation, I listen to her tell him about all the changes being made, the ones that have already taken place and how this won't be a hotel for sex soon enough.

"How can you re-open a hotel that hasn't closed down yet?" he laughs, not taking her words seriously. "And how are you going to stop people from having sex in your rooms? What are you going to do, spy on your guests or something?" he adds, finding it all very funny.

You will be laughing on the other side of your face when this place is finished, Gary. Wow, how I wish I could become unprofessional for just a couple of seconds and

41

give him...

"How dare you mock our hotel, Sir?" Jenna suddenly growls at him, totally out of character. "If you don't like the rules and don't appreciate our service, I suggest you find somewhere else to stay tonight" she adds red with rage, full of surprise and seemingly waiting for an apology.

"Oh come on girls, you know I don't stay here all night long anyway" he continues to mock. "I'm in, out, shake it all about, then I leave this shit-hole and return to my mansion" he adds, waiting to be given his key-card.

"Out!" demands Jenna, adamantly pointing her finger towards the main door.

Did we err... Did we turn into a classy hotel already? Is the getting rid of the nasty guests already taking place then? Seriously, I don't know what's happening right now. Did we let old Mr Hodge in, or was I just dreaming this part?

"Why don't you come to my room in about half an hour, and we'll see what I can do about that mood of yours" he laughs once again, snatching the key-card from Jenna's hand.

"Christina, call the police" she barks, instructing me to do something I've never done in this hotel before.

"Err, Okay then" I confusingly respond, picking up the phone, realizing Jenna is making a statement and I must stick with my colleague no matter how weird it feels.

As I hold the phone in my hand, strangely forgetting which number to dial for the police, Gary then gives me a daring look, then quickly backs down.

"Okay, okay, I'm sorry" he starts to sing out. "Just give me my room and I will never darken your magnificent hotel again" he adds, still with a hint of sarcasm in his voice, I fear.

"Fine" Jenna snaps at him, snatching the key-card back from his playful hands. "But first, you enter the room you always soil, then clean the place up" she demands.

Wow, look at his face now. He doesn't know if to laugh at her, agree or cry. Saying that, how am I feeling standing here, knowing I'm about to become a manageress, yet I'm useless in this type of situation?

"Fuck off" he decides to laugh. "I'm not cleaning that room. I pay to use it, not clean my spunk off the ceiling" he adds, trying to snatch the key-card back from her.

With that Jenna moves her hand, smiles, then points over to the main door again.

"Then your kind of custom isn't welcome here any longer" she tells him.

A snigger, an unsure smile, then a frown all appear on Gary's face, before he finally realizes she's deadly serious. With that he turns, mumbles something under his breath, then starts his long shameful exit. Just as he reaches the door, Bill Hodge's door opens and out he comes carrying his chair. Damn it... I forgot to tape my note to his door before all of...

"Mr Hodge, please take your chair back into your room" Jenna calls out, like a nineteen year old, going on a head teacher in her sixties.

"B... b... but I always s... sit out here" he responds, kind of shocked, if his always blank expression can be considered shocked.

"If you'd like to sit in reception, there are new seats available, otherwise stay in your room" she calls out.

Although I totally agree on how Jenna is putting our only guest in his place, I do happen to feel she's being a little too harsh with all her new found power, so give her a light playful nudge.

"I know, I know, but I've got to do it" she whispers with a secret smile at me.

As we watch Mr Hodge reluctantly place his chair back inside his room and slowly stagger towards the new seating area and us at the desk. I don't know if it's the new snob in me, but now he's coming over, I don't actually think I want him sitting his dirty clothing on our lovely new...

"Aha, b.... b.... bugger it" he grunts, realizing the new seating area isn't to his liking. "This hotel is... is g... going downhill" he grumbles, heading back into his room and slamming the door shut.

10:54pm (Tuesday 23rd March)

Although the hotel is changing before my very eyes and new attitudes are forming faster than the furniture is settling out of it's wrapping, nothing prepares me for this time of night, where I predict Jenna is about to disappear and Mr Hodge is going to ring through for his 11 o'clock drink. As usual, the minute I fear it coming, the second I start to think about it, the phone rings, yet for a change Jenna is still sitting at the desk with me.

"Cure Hotel, Jenna speaking, how can I help you?" she says, shocking me a little more by answering the phone herself. "No Mr Hodge, room service isn't available at this moment in time" she tells him, before wishing him a pleasant night, then hanging up.

Feeling a little gobsmacked, I want to speak, but I don't know what to say to her.

"I don't know what's going on around here tonight,

44

but I kind of like it" I confusingly whisper, with a huge grin.

"We start as we mean to go on" she responds, explaining whether the changes came tonight, tomorrow or next week, we had to introduce them at some point, so why not now?

With Gary Sheen refused a room tonight and Bill Hodge stopped from sitting and watching us, or having his creepy room service request delivered, I'm in a really good mood, so suggest Jenna take her break an hour earlier than normal.

"We've only got Mr Hodge staying tonight, so I don't think I need a break" she answers, claiming sitting at this new desk is all the break she needs. "You go for yours, if you want" she then adds.

Please someone other than Mr Hodge, pinch me. Because although I've seen Jenna in a good mood before, this is a crazy good mood!

After telling her I'd rather wait until 1 o'clock for my break and admit that I'm feeling a little frisky tonight, we continue to sit at the desk together, with not much else to do. Suddenly, it happens...

"Oh, I didn't tell you what happened between Greg and I this morning, did I?"

Oh no... How do I tell her I will take that break two seconds after refusing it, knowing what's coming now?

"No, you didn't tell me. What happened?" I respond, trying to do my best impression of being interested.

Here we go then – Brace yourself Christina!

"When I got home this morning, Greg wasn't actually there" she tells me, starting off her story.

Okay... In the year I've been forced to listen to these stories, never has this guy called Greg never not been there, so I'm listening.

"He actually walked in five minutes after me, then surprised me with news that he's taking the week off work"

Okay... This has now got to be the most boring story you've ever told me, and there have been a few!

"For the first time in ages, we didn't, you know? We didn't do anything in the morning"

It's official... This is the most boring story she's ever told, read me or made up for conversation.

"He promised me, we were about to embark on a whole week of new exciting stuff"

Really? What like having an orgasm or... Wait a minute...

"Jenna, why after all this time hearing stories about you and Greg and I never heard you say the word sex?" I ask for some unknown reason.

"What are you talking about Christina, of course I've said that word" she answers, blushing.

"Go on then" I dare her. "Say a rude word right now" I add, keeping it friendly, yet knowing something strange is bothering me now.

"No" she nervously giggles.

"Say something" I egg her on, giggling too.

As the playful spat continues between us, it's all very harmless until I apparently push her too hard.

"Seriously Christina, I don't want to speak like that" she tells me again, looking more worried about it now.

"Come on Jenna" I continue giggling. "Say sex, or orgasm. Anything rude" I push, not that I call this pushing myself.

With that she pushes her new chair backwards, stands

up, then claims she's going for a break after all.

"Jenna, I was only messing about" I call out, as she storms off upstairs, ignoring my apology.

Wow, that turned strangely intense, didn't it? What's wrong with her? I was only having a...

"Y... y.... you shouldn't t.... tease her like t... that"

FUCK ME! If I wanted to work in the haunted house down at the fairground, I would have taken a job there. Why does this weird guy keep making me leap out of my skin? In-fact, I'm sure I just peed a little then.

"What did you say, Mr Hodge?" I call out, finally spotting him outside his door, sitting on his bloody chair. Should I warn him that Jenna won't be pleased if she sees him with it? Why not, I'm a manageress too now, aren't I?

"T... that's why I... I made sure she... she had gone first" he tells me.

Great, I'm the push-over manageress now, am I?

"Be... be..."

Yes Mr Hodge, be, be, be what? Come on, get it out and leave me alone.

"Be... beware of the quiet ones C... Christina" he grumbles, before picking up his chair and disappearing back into his room again.

Beware? Beware? What the hell did that mean? Would it have been so scary if it wasn't him actually saying it?

12:42 am (Wednesday 24th March)

It's now approaching time for my break and although Jenna had her little tantrum just after eleven, I haven't seen her since. Yes, I've been sitting here wondering where she disappears to; considering I can see most of the hotel now the lights are all working, but it's my break time, so who cares? Yes, I've also freaked out a few times about what Mr Hodge said, but as I said, it's break time. In-fact, it's break time, break time, break time, break – And if Jenna doesn't return soon, I'm going to miss it and possibly miss out on the quickie I've been planning all night long. I want my break now!

12:48 am (Wednesday 24th March)

"Come on, come on. Where are you Jenna?"

12:52 am (Wednesday 24th March)

"Seriously Jenna, if you don't hurry up, I'm going to call out your name, wake Mr Hodge, then you're going to be here all on your own with him"

12:58 am (Wednesday 24th March)

"Okay Christina, off you go. Enjoy your break" Jenna says, suddenly appearing just like a ghost at the top of the metal stairs.

Now isn't the time to be asking her where she's been. In-fact, I'm not even waiting for her to reach the bottom of the stairs, because I'm out of here. I can't risk her putting a downer on what I've been building up in my head and knickers for the last hour. It's time to go and find myself a little bit of fun for an hour!

Tuesday night, not exactly anything happening out here on the streets, is there? Wow, if it's this dead over at the bar tonight, I might just have to make barman Dean's naughty dreams come true. Oh no, come on... What's going on now? Why is the bar door locked?

"DEAN... DEAN" I call out, banging on the door, knowing in the whole year I've been coming here, this place has never been closed.

Wow, I hope nothing has happened to Dean. I hope everything is okay. Hold on – What's this?

Dear Christina,
Sorry, I've closed early. I wanted to go and check out this new bar. See you tomorrow morning. Enjoy the drink I've left for you in the mail box.
Dean x

Seriously? Closing early – Rude. Offering me no men on a night like this – Dangerous. Leaving me a drink and this note – I will let him off, I guess. Now, where is this sodding drink?

7:52 am (Wednesday 24ᵗʰ March)

"Christina, Christina, wake up"

"Christina, come on. Mr Harper will be here in a few minutes"

Okay, what happened? Wow, did I just say that out loud?

"Your friend closed the bar early this morning, but left you a bottle of something alcoholic" she tells me, in her prudish nuns voice. "You decided to have one, two or six, then passed out on our new comfy seats" she adds.

That's right... I wanted to calm my frustrated knickers by having a drink, didn't I? Then I wanted to try out the new seats. Wow, I must have fallen...

"Come on Christina, he's about to walk in. I don't want you to get into trouble or lose your job" Jenna panics in my ear.

And this is why you are my friend here at work, Jenna. Despite the weird sulking thing you do, you are actually a really nice person.

"What's this then girls, sleeping on the job?" chirps Mr Harper, walking in to admire the changes we've made overnight, yet noticing me sprawled across the seating area more.

Shit... I'm about to be fired, aren't I?

"I let Christina have a few hours sleep, because she worked on the reception area all night long, whilst I dealt with a troubled guest" Jenna quickly explains, having an instant plan to save my ass.

"Well it sounds like you've both had a busy night, so I won't hold you up" Mr Harper responds, claiming the place looks amazing. "See you both tonight" he adds, waving us off.

CHAPTER 3 - *LATE*

If being drunk at work after just being promoted, then nearly getting caught sleeping by Mr Harper wasn't bad enough, at this exact moment in time I find myself leaping out of bed at a quarter to eight, slightly hungover. Why didn't my alarm wake me up at five-thirty this evening? Why did Dean have to leave me that bottle of alcohol outside his bar? Why do I do such stupid things? Why can't I be more like Jenna?

Clearly not best pleased with myself, I race into my bathroom, where I know a quick shower is required, because I'm already going to be late for work and now it's a simple case of damage control. Just then as I soak my body under the hot stream of water, it all comes flooding back to me... I drank at one this morning because I didn't find myself a man, when I needed one to please me, didn't I? And now it's day three without an orgasm in sight, I just know I'm going to act like a crazy nymphomaniac all night long, aren't I? Seriously, if I didn't just wake up feeling so tired, I think I would be abusing the lower half of my body right now under this shower. Cor, I felt so horny yesterday I could have humped the leg off our new desk, so god knows what I'm going to be feeling tonight, once I get myself going. Saying that, yes I do... I'm going to sleep with anyone, aren't I? Sometimes I scare myself heading into one of these sexual moods, but at least the sex I have at the end of it is going to be amazing and... Shit, stop stalling Christina, haven't you realized you're late already?

Oh well, it's eight forty-three and if I didn't already know it, I'm arriving at work late. Not that I actually thought I'd be on time, because I randomly decided to follow a hot guy in and out of the train station, hoping to get lucky on the way here. Wow, look at this... In-fact, am I actually standing outside the hotel I work at? Once again it looks like Mr Harper has pulled out all the stops today, because this place looks like a hotel at last. The vacancy sign that has been propped up the window, giving off the only sign this place is a hotel over the years has gone, and now a huge neon sign shines out with the Cure Hotel written on it. The front door has been painted and the windows have been cleaned, if not replaced, because I can't actually remember what they looked like before now. This is it – The place in which I finally start a career worth having – The place that is going to help me grow up and turn into a mature young woman – Once I've fucked someone's brains out tonight, of course!

As I walk into the impressive looking building, it's as though I forgot all about the new furniture in the reception area and I'm quickly surprised again noticing it. Wow, I actually work here, don't I?

"I had a feeling you were going to be late in this evening" beams Jenna behind our desk, welcoming me onto the start of my shift.

"Sorry Jenna, I'm really..."

"It's okay Christina, don't worry about it, I covered for you" she quickly sings out, not giving me the chance to panic or apologize, claiming she told Mr Harper that I was at a dental appointment, before asking me how it went.

"How what went?" I confusingly respond, walking over to the desk, grateful she has covered for me yet again.

"The dentist, Silly" she giggles at me. "Wow, I hope you're more convincing in the morning, when Mr Harper questions you about it" she adds.

Is this like one of her romantic tales about Greg, where she actually thinks I've been to the dentist because she's just made it up, or is she trying to be funny? Damn, I really can't tell, but dread upsetting her this soon, especially as she's just saved my ass twice in the last twenty-four hours.

Instead of getting into the fictional dentist visit story with her, I decide to ask who's checked in tonight.

"Mr Hodge is in room three" she tells me.

"No Gary Sheen tonight then?" I ask, deciding to do my professional receptionist bit, before letting my mind wander, then hoping he'd come in to be my last sexual resort if needed tonight.

"No Gary and no more room either" she answers, claiming rooms 1, 2 and 4 downstairs are now closed to the public, as requested by Mike Harper himself.

"What happens when Mr Harper is working on the final room and we've got no rooms to offer visitors tomorrow night?" I quickly ask, realizing something is bothering me, yet the number one receptionist around here must know the answer.

"The final room will close in the morning, then we're officially open for business with all of the other new rooms" she explains, quite excited by this.

See... I knew she'd know the answer. Oh well, seeing as Mr Hodge has taken the only room we've got tonight, I guess I'm going to have to find my fun across the street at Dean's bar later on.

"As of tomorrow night, seven of our eight rooms will be open to the public at a rate of one hundred dollars per night, then in a few weeks time, I will be heading off into the new day time shift" she continues to explain, telling me things that I obviously missed from Mr Harper himself, being late in.

Wow, I actually forgot about that. I'm going to be night shift manageress, aren't I? I'm going to be allowed to hire three employees, aren't I? MM-mm, I wonder if I could hire a male stripper for my own sexual pleasure, when my knickers are doing cartwheels on nights like these?

"Oh and Mr Harper was a little disappointed about your dentist visit, because he desperately wanted to show you something else tonight"

Tell me it was his penis. Oh go on, tell me...

"He not only finished the outside of the building today, but he managed to..."

"He finished my little nightclub, didn't he?" I cut her

short, leaving her at the desk and running over to the door, straight away realizing I'm going to look completely mental if I'm wrong.

As I worry about getting it wrong, then grown-up Jenna walks over as though she's my mom going to let me open my birthday presents early, she tells me to open the door.

"HOLY SHIT!" I scream, unable to believe my eyes.

Right in front of me is a multicolored dance floor, with one of those disco balls hanging from the ceiling in the middle of it. Over in the corner, a lime green bar, with drinks, drinks and more drinks on top of it, obviously ready to be put away or consumed by me. The walls are all painted yellow, with funny shapes on them.

"Two questions" I quickly say, realizing there could well be more, but for now there's only two. "Why the weird walls and where's the music?" I ask.

I mean, what's the point having a little nightclub, if there's no music?

"Close the door, Christina" she says.

Why is she so calm? Why isn't she excited like I am?

"HOLY SHIT!" I scream out again, as she presses a little button on a control pad on the wall, then really loud dance music pumps out from everywhere. "HOLY SHIT!" I then gasp, as I watch her press another one and all the lights kick into action too. "No way" I gasp for a third time, as I watch my professional uptight friend then take to the dance floor and start shaking her skinny little ass.

Although I know drinking, dancing and loud music are more my thing, I just can't believe my eyes, as Jenna lets go on the dance floor and really shakes it. In-fact wow, she's actually quite a good dancer!

If none of this wasn't mind blowing enough, what I then do next probably blows my mind more than anything, because I can't believe I'm about to do it. I walk across to the control pad on the wall and turn the music down like the grown-up I didn't think I was. More mind blowing? Jenna now shaking her thing on the dance floor is giving me strange looks, as if to ask why have I just spoiled her fun.

"Have you forgotten, Mr Hodge is in the hotel?" I quickly question her, claiming the noise in this room could wake the dead.

"The weird yellow walls are sound proof, Christina. Which means you wouldn't be able to hear the music, even if you placed your ear to the door outside" she explains.

With that, I turn it up even louder, instantly wanting to test out her theory. I open the door, step outside, then listen. Wow, not a peep from the room inside. I then open the door again and confirm it works, before standing in the doorway, admiring our little nightclub.

"Y... you y... y... young ones are horrible. Y... you should be... be ashamed of y... y... yourselves" grunts Mr Hodge coming out of his room to have a go at us, then slamming his door shut again.

"I thought you said this room was sound proof?" I confusingly question, as Mr Hodge's shiver of death races up my spine after he's gone.

"Not when somebody keeps opening the door and letting the music out" laughs Jenna.

If this lovely surprise wasn't the cherry on the cake already for me, Jenna has one final surprise before we head back to our desk. She walks over to the bar, where the drinks are almost reaching the ceiling, then hits another button on the key pad.

"Oh no. No, he didn't" I gasp for the one hundredth time.

There above the bar is another neon sign, which apparently gives the bar its name.

"He wanted to call this room Jentina, as a way of thanking us for all of our loyalty" she explains.

As a single tear falls from my eye and I choke up a little too, it's here I realize - I've never been treated this way before. Yes, I have many people in my life that like me, but never have I been appreciated like this and dare I say it, I want it a lot more!

As Jenna closes the door behind her, then uncovers the sign on the outside of the door too, the surprises just keep on coming...

Jentina Nightclub
Guests $10 per night – Visitors $20

I can't believe this. I thought this little club was going to be exclusive to hotel guests, but it seems anyone can come here of an evening – This is going to be insane! Only yesterday I could actually vision the mental ideas Mr Harper had for this place that I couldn't see before, but now I can see it all. This place is going to become a little gold mine. I could bring all my friends here to make a profit, then if they wanted to stay over, give them a discount on a room. Seriously, I'm going to love and worship this place every single day from now on.

"There's one thing you aren't going to like, that I'd better tell you about now" Jenna says, once we're back at the desk and I haven't taken my eyes off the Jentina nightclub sign yet.

You could tell me anything right now Jenna and it wouldn't bother me – Trust me, nothing could bring me down right now.

9:10pm (Wednesday 24ᵗʰ March)

"Our new uniforms turned up" she tells me.

Is that it? I don't care, I'd wear anything to work here. In-fact, I'd welcome the guests in naked if it meant keeping my job now! As I watch her reach behind the desk and pull out the plastic covering my new outfit, I'm ready for it. In-fact, I can't wait to try it on and wear it with pride.

"Mr Harper wants to turn up in the morning and see us wearing them" she tells me, handing mine over.

"So why aren't you wearing yours already then?" I quickly question, noticing she's still wearing the skirt she hates wearing, with those black tights.

"Just try it on and be wearing it in the morning" she tells me, heading off somewhere.

"Where are you going?" I call out, obviously knowing Jenna does her disappearing act from time to time, but never this early in the evening.

She tells me that Mr Harper has asked her to check the secret passages, then do a little work on the new control pads going into the rooms.

"Control pads?" I question, not having a clue what she's talking about.

"Remember when we were standing in the new room? Remember you noticed the hole in the wall?" she quickly reminds me.

"Oh that's right. The pad that's going to control the

curtains, the TV and the lights" I answer, remembering my version of a glory hole on the wall now.

"I will be about an hour or so, so try on your new uniform and keep an eye on the desk" she calls out, disappearing into the secret passage door, which leads to walkways behind the rooms I've never seen before.

Oh well, that's her gone, so let's see what Mr Harper expects us to wear to work every day, shall we? MM-mm, a light blue blouse, yet more modern looking than this white one I have on now. Yeah, can still do something with my cleavage in this. Oh and dark blue trousers, what a joy – I bet Jenna is made-up about this? Okay Christina, you can do this – Just because he doesn't want our legs shown off any longer, doesn't mean you can't tighten these things up and use your ass instead. Yeah, I can wear this, I can't pull this look off. Now where should I try it on? Certainly not out here. Don't want Mr Hodge coming out to spy on me, do I?

As I weigh up my options, but all I can think about is my little nightclub Jentina, I quickly have an idea. If I take the key-card to closed off room number four, I could get changed in there quickly, whilst keeping an eye on the front door too. Without any delay I grab the key-card, throw my new outfit over my shoulder, then head to room four quickly. I've chosen room number four because it's the room we've hired out the least, so isn't that dirty. Saying that, if Mr Harper has closed room one; where Gary Sheen used to stay with his prostitute friends, maybe he's renovated it already? No harm in me changing in there if he has, is there? I throw room fours key-card on the desk, then grab room ones pass instead,

59

quickly making my way over. If someone walks in to book a room now, they'll ring the bell on the desk, won't they? Saying that, with Mr Hodge staying in the only room we have available tonight, we've got no room at the inn anyway, have we?

9:16pm (Wednesday 24ᵗʰ March)

Here goes then... Key-card to the lock... Has Mr Harper transformed this room, or am I still going to smell Gary's stale overused aftershave in here?

"Wow" I gasp for the two hundredth time tonight, noticing this room now looks like the finished ones upstairs.

The bed looks amazingly comfortable - The flat screen TV clearly hasn't been used, because it's not wired up to the glory hole in the wall yet – Wow, this room is amazing!

"I want to live here" I sigh to myself, quickly closing the door behind me.

Go on Christina, try out the bed. No, have a look in the bathroom first. No, bounce on the bed, because no-one has ever had sex on it before. Saying that, hitch up your skirt, masturbate, then cum all over the fresh sheets. Yeah, that will work and also take some of this sexual tension out of my body. No Christina, have some respect, Mr Harper has worked really hard in here today, so don't go messing it up. That's right, take out your new uniform, put it on, then have your little bit of sex across the street tonight instead.

As I drop my old skirt to the floor and onto the new carpet no-one has ever stood on before, I take a look at it massaging my toes. Who the hell puts on purple spotty knickers, when she's out to have sex? Oh that's right, me when I'm late for work and rushing to get dressed. Okay, off comes the old top and on goes the new one. Wow, this feels kind of nice, now where's the... Note to self – Remind me to suggest Mr Harper put up some mirrors in his rooms, because girls need mirrors to sort out there cleavage. Okay, let's move this into the bathroom, I noticed yesterday that the upstairs rooms have huge mirrors in their bathrooms. Pick up your new trousers, then that's right, forget about masturbating on that lovely new bed and finish what you came in here for – To get dressed. Now Christina, when you get in there, don't get excited with the new marble interior, just get...

"HOLY SHIT!"

"Who the hell are you?" I gasp, as some random guy steps out of the shower, as soon as I enter the room.

Oh my god, he can see my disgusting purple knickers, can't he? What are you talking about Christina, you can see his everything! No, now you can't, because he's just grabbed a towel and covered it all up. Wow, why can I still see his penis, even though he's covered it with that towel? Okay, turn into the professional manageress you are and refrain from cumin in your pants right now. Shit... Knickers... He's still looking at them, isn't he? Quick, grab the other towel and cover up too.

"Sir, I don't know how you got in here or what you're doing, but these rooms are closed to the public" I tell him, standing like the professional manageress I am, clutching a small towel, covering the lower half of my body.

"It's okay, it's okay, I'm..." he starts to explain.

"Oh, are you a relative of Mr Harper, the owner?" I ask

him, assuming that's what he was going to say, hoping he agrees, which would then make this situation that little bit more passable in my head.

"Yes I am. I am a relative of Mr Harper" he answers, as his wet bare chest shines right into my eyes. "But where's the other girl, Jenna?" he asks.

Oh, Jenna knows you're staying, does she? She must have forgotten to tell me about you then. Yeah right, more kept it a secret, because she'd know what I'd do to him! Oops, there goes my unprofessional mind again and there goes my towel. Why did I just drop it on the floor? Why is he now looking at my purple knickers again? Okay, this is not awkward, it's dead sexy. Make this happen for yourself Christina, find a way of sleeping with a good looking guy in this hotel for once. Wow, how that new bed seems really appealing now?

"So, Jenna knows you're staying here, does she?" I ask, suddenly feeling the need to bite on my bottom lip and cross my legs seductively against the sink area.

"Yes, I think I spoke to her as I arrived" he answers, clearly trying to work out why I haven't picked up my towel again, or what naughty things I'm thinking up for him to do to me.

Fair enough, not every guy in the world is going to remember having a conversation on arrival with Jenna. Wow, I don't remember half the conversations I have with her and I work here.

"So, what do you think of your Uncles? Father's new room then?" I question him, guessing at how he's related to Mr Harper.

Last thing I need to do is sleep with someone in his family, then piss him off and lose my job.

"Err, Uncle, yeah he's my Uncle. Second Uncle on my

mother's side" he responds, seemingly nervous of my questioning all of a sudden.

"And what do you think of the new bed next door?" I ask, deciding to go in for the kill, leaning myself against the door, knowing he's going to have to brush his semi naked body past mine to look.

As it happens, as our bodies almost lock together in the small door way, he looks deep into my eyes and tells me the bed looks nice.

"And would you believe, they've never been fucked in before" I whisper, looking up at him, with a take me message written in my pupils.

With that I extend my neck and plant my lips against his, then pull away his towel. Instantly I'm impressed because I can feel his wet erection jab against my body, so I know he's up for this too. As he seems quite shocked by my directness and when our lips finally do come apart, I grab hold of his hand to pull him towards the bed, falling on the bed myself, making sure his sexy body follows. For a man on top of a woman only wearing a blouse and a pair of purple knickers, I would imagine he would go nuts at this stage, but he still seems to be holding off slightly, so I reach down and grab at his erection, then start tugging at it slightly.

"I want you inside me, right now" I whisper, letting go of his shaft a few seconds later, removing my knickers whilst he's still on top of...

"Sorry, sorry, I can't... I can't do this" he suddenly panics, leaping up, leaving my naked body exposed alone on the bed.

"It's okay, I won't tell anyone. You haven't got to worry about your Uncle" I tell him, knowing my insides are turning over, my vagina is doing cartwheels and his naked wet body across the room looks eatable.

"I... I... I need to talk to Jenna" he then shocks me by saying.

What is it about this guy and his fascination with Jenna? What - Does he feel he needs to run it past her first or something? Let me tell you Mister, she'd never agree, especially in one of these new rooms.

"Jenna's busy at the moment, but just like her, I'm the manageress of this hotel, so I can help you with anything you need" I tell him, making my seductive move across the room.

Normally in this situation, where a man isn't taking me when I'm throwing all my best moves at him, I would have got the hump by now, but this guy is different, he is the challenge I crave. He's refreshingly nervous, he's clearly shaking and fuck, it's making me want him so much more!

"Come with me, I won't hurt you" I whisper, taking his hand once again, then leading him back towards the bed.

As he reluctantly follows, I lie him down on top of it, so his nervous shaft is standing up in the air. With that I slowly join him, mount his shaking body, then begin to lower myself down on top of him.

"Seriously, we shouldn't be doing this" he whispers looking up at me, as I slowly begin my descent.

Which means in the language of Christina, that he's about to cave in and give up resisting, because he wouldn't be lying here saying it, if he didn't want this to happen too. As I feel the very top of him enter me, yet I hold it a little longer to let my oncoming tightening emerge, this is it – The moment I'm about to have sex in this hotel and have a guy I really like the look...

"Please, no, don't do it" he begins to beg, looking

really worried.

"Really? You don't want to feel this on top of you then?" I playfully tease, realizing he's saying the words, yet his pelvis has started to lift off the bed underneath me, because he does want to feel me submerge it.

"I do, I do, but only with Jenna. Only with Jenna" he squeals, as I ease down, instantly feeling him throb inside me and...

"Excuse me?" I then shudder, as I quickly hop off the bed, trying to work out what he's trying to say. "You'd rather sleep with Jenna than me?" I question, pulling all kinds of strange faces at him, whilst...

Holy shit, this is Greg, isn't it? Hold on, how is Greg related to Mr Harper then? Wow, that would explain why he's acting like a virgin, wouldn't it?

"What's your name?" I quickly ask, picking up the towel I made him drop, as I cover myself up.

"Greg" he answers, confirming my worst fear.

Shit... I've just seductively slid down Jenna's boyfriend's penis, haven't I? Oh my god, she's going to...

"Why did you tell me you were related to Mr Harper then?" I quickly question again, as he sits up pulling the fresh new duvet over himself.

"Because I didn't want to get Jenna in trouble for sneaking me in here" he announces, starting to look worried again.

"I think sneaking you in and getting her in trouble should be the last thing you worry about right now" I tell him. "If she finds us in here together, she will kill us both" I add, as a sense of fear, naughty excitement and terror floods my body all at the same time.

As he listens to what I'm saying then leaps off the bed, I watch as he races through into the bathroom to find his clothes. I quickly follow knowing my uniform is in there too and before we know it, we're both standing half naked, or naked again in his case, in the same small room.

"You know, we could..."

Don't even think about it Greggy-boy. You had your chance with me and you blew it. It's no good looking at me getting dressed, deciding you want a piece of my ass now.

"So what was the plan?" I quickly ask, pulling up my new trousers.

"Plan?" he responds, still looking at me with lustful thoughts racing through his mind.

"The plan. The plan between you and Jenna?" I huff at him, claiming he needs to snap out of it, if we're going to get away with this.

"But we didn't do anything" he panics, the second I've said it.

Why are men so stupid? Oh who am I kidding, this is Jenna's partner we're talking about here. If he's as backwards as her, he's going to believe sex only occurs between a couple when they romantically cum together. Me sliding down onto his penis, although it only happened for a few seconds, won't be considered sex in his head, will it?

"She was going to take her break, then join me in this room" he finally tells me.

"Then that's what is going to happen" I respond, rushing through into the bedroom again, straightening the bed, then telling him I was never here.

As I wish him luck, demand he doesn't fuck this up, I take a final look at the man that never was, then slowly open the door.

"Really Christina?" Jenna suddenly says the second I open it, standing outside looking furious.
Oh shit!

"Taking care of one of your fancy men in a new room we're banned from, are you?" she asks, shaking her head in a disapproving way.
Okay, I'm now officially confused. If she secretly checked Greg into this room and knows he's in here waiting for her, why would she ask this? That's if she doesn't know I know it's Greg and she's testing me. Damn, I've got to say something, haven't I?

"I... I... I was going to use this room to try on my new uniform, because I didn't want to do it in reception" I start to explain.
Yeah that sounds good, keep going. What are you talking about Christina? Of course it sounds good, that's the bloody truth.

"Then as I walked in, I met Greg, the man you've secretly - Naughty, naughty, given a room to for the night, so I'm coming back out again" I add, shaking my head in a disapproving way too.
Suddenly, it all flips in my favor.

"You aren't going to say anything to Mr Harper, are you?" she panics a little, showing me I've just got away with it, as long as Greg doesn't blab.

"Jenna, you've had my back many times over the twelve or so months we've worked together. Now it's my turn to have your back" I tell her, claiming I only wish she had told me before I was surprised by a random naked man in the bathroom, before complimenting her on a man well found and further more, not a fictional character from a novel.

11:11pm (Wednesday 24ᵗʰ March)

I don't know how I got away with that earlier, but I'm so glad Jenna didn't find out. Yes, I let a sense of lying bitch guilt race through my mind about an hour ago, but I got over it. I wish I had got off on it now, considering he's the first man to ever penetrate me and not finish things off. Jenna entered the room an hour and twenty minutes ago and hasn't been seen since. In-fact, she entered the room as soon as I left and although I say I haven't seen her since, I've definitely heard her. Wow, for someone so prudish and backwards about sex, she sure knows how to shout about it. In-fact, I did consider locking myself in Jentina about half an hour ago, just so I wouldn't be able to hear them going at it any longer. I tell you what, that girl has stamina, because if it was me in there with him, I would have been done, showered and onto my next man by now, but still she's going.

"MM-mm yeah, just like that" I hear her scream.

I don't know what he's doing to her in there, but he's been getting it right for the last twenty minutes, or so I can work out. It's weird because although only a couple of days ago at this time of night, I would be fearing Mr Hodge's coke request, I'd quite happily hear him stutter at me now, just to blank out the noises my trusty colleague is making. God, I hope she isn't making a mess in that new room, so Mr Harper finds out someone's been entertaining in there, because I don't think I would be able to cover it up. I say cover it up, but I don't think he'd believe it was Jenna in there and not me.

"MM-mm yeah, right there, right there"

I give Jenna the credit she deserves, because she's heard me do this loads in the past, but did I expect her to be so vocal? I think not! Saying that, I still haven't heard her say anything rude, sexual or dirty yet, have I? Hey, maybe that's why I'm still listening.

"My pussy, my pussy. My pussy is going to explode!"
Okay, I was wrong, I have heard her say something rude!

"Do you think Christina can hear us?" I hear her call out.
Hey, don't bring me into your sex life, Jenna. Wow, I really think Mr Harper should have made his walls a lot thicker when refurbishing these rooms.

"I hope she can, because it would really turn me on" she continues to scream.
And now I've heard her say something sexual, yet a little bit kinky too. This is amazing, I think?

"MM-mm, yeah, she can hear us" I then hear Greg respond.
Okay, that question from her definitely turned him on, because I can now hear the headboard being bashed even harder. Careful there Greg, don't think about me too much, or you might stupidly confess I sat on top of you earlier on.

"HERE IT COMES!"
Seriously guys, calm down, you're making me really wet out here! Break, break, when is my fucking break time? I want my break, so a guy over at the bar can break me in two!

11:26pm (Wednesday 24ᵗʰ March)

It's all gone quiet in room number one at last. I'm actually surprised Mr Hodge hasn't been out to complain up until now. Anyway, thank god that's over! Saying that, I was feeling a little uptight about hearing Jenna the fantasy story-teller having sex tonight, but now it's stopped, I find myself quickly hoping they start up again. Not because their noises are turning me on; because they are, but just because I fear her coming out soon and having to face her. I mean, what do you say to a woman you thought was a virgin all this time? Well done? Did you enjoy that? Wow, now thinking about it, what did Jenna say to me when I emerged from the same disgusting room a few weeks back? Oh that's right, finished? Yeah, let's go with that then – Finished.

"Finished, have you?" I find myself asking all of two seconds later, as she comes out of the room, looking like hell fire has stormed down on her and peed in her eye.

"Not yet. I just need a drink of water" she casually responds, walking over towards me, picking up the key-card for another room, claiming the drinking water isn't running in her room.

"Oh..." I answer, not having the words to say to her after all.

As I watch her disappear into the next room with an empty cup, I quickly notice she's left her door open. MM-mm, penis on a bed – Penis on a bed, vacant – Penis on a bed vacant, that wanted me a few hours ago.

"Go on Christina, quickly" I egg myself on quietly, not wanting to do anything sinister, but just have a look.

As soon as I've found the courage to lift my buttocks off my seat, Jenna's racing back out of the other room, claiming one more round of sex and I will be able to go for my break.

"Yeah, err, okay then..." I respond, unable to believe what I'm seeing in my former prudish friend, as I suddenly notice she's racing around out here without any knickers on.

11:31pm **(Wednesday 24ᵗʰ March)**

Come on Christina, stop being such a prude – Go over there and find out if there's a crack in the door or something. Fair enough, I'm not actually into watching people; considering I'm more a doer than a viewer, but listen to these noises again. I just want to make sure she's not behind that door alone, he's gone home and this is another of the tales she's going to tell me tomorrow night.

As I creep over towards the door, the first thing I can feel is the tightening of these new trousers. How the hell did I get into them so fast earlier? Did I really have to get into them, considering I don't think it would have mattered if Jenna walked in on us now?

"Do you fancy my friend Christina?" I can hear Jenna ask, as I place my ear to their door. "Show me how much you'd like to have sex with her right now" she adds, as Greg apparently gives it to her hard again.

"Aah, he does like me – That's nice!" I sing out quietly to myself.

Noticing that there's no crack in the door, under it or over it, I decide to give up and return to my desk before I'm caught spying on my friend. Who would have thought it, me a spying pervert? No sooner am I half way back to my desk, when I feel my key-card smack me in the leg and give me a crazy idea. I head back towards the door with a small plan, then slide my key-card inside it. The door unlocks, I push it open slowly, then I see what I've been tempting myself to see all this time...

When the hell did she wheel her desk chair through into this room? Why is my brunette friend sitting on it naked, rolling around the room? And more to the point, why is Greg now on the floor, being spanked by what looks to be a plastic ruler by her? Wow, Jenna's a freak and...

"Can I help you, Christina?" I hear Jenna ask, forgetting they might see me with my head around the door like this.

Wow, did she just spin towards me on that chair? Did I really just see her neatly trimmed... Yes I did and I've just seen it again, err?...

"I'm heading off for my break now" I whisper, thinking up the fool proof plan I had ready in my head.

"No problem. See you later" she responds, waiting for me to leave, seemingly unfazed by my intrusion. "Don't do anything I wouldn't do" she calls out, as I close the door again.

What exactly wouldn't you do Jenna? Because I've seriously seen you in a different light tonight!

11:36pm (Wednesday 24th March)

"Wow, you're in early this evening, aren't you Christina?" Dean calls out behind his bar, with another two men propping it up on my side.

"Hello Sexy, fancy a drink?" one of the tipsy guys ask, looking me up and down in my new uniform.

"You know what..." I respond towards the rude guy. "Forget the drink and have me instead" I add, grabbing him by the hand, then yanking him off his bar stool.

"Be careful with her Thomas, she's an animal" calls Dean playfully, knowing exactly where I'm taking him.

Without a single word and letting him feel all his

Christmas's have come at once, I lead him into the female toilets and pin him against the sink. I lunge at him like I have done to other men in the past, but not so dedicated to the mission I'm currently on. This guy isn't as hot as Jenna's man, but who cares? If he can get it up right now, it will make me happy!

"So, do you do this..." he tries to say, as I press my hand to his lips, then start unzipping his jeans.
Suddenly, something happens to me that's never happened before – I lose interest. Obviously, I don't give up on myself, so kiss him with my tongue and grope at his hardening shaft for a few seconds but again, I've lost it. It's as though Jenna and stupid Greg have flooded my mind so much, that this empty casual sex I've been having for so long, means nothing to...

"I'm sorry, I can't do this" I tell him, pulling away as his hands start to wander up and down my body.

"Oh yes you can" he grunts at me, rubbing his hand right against the inside of my legs, pulling me closer again with force.

"NO, I CAN'T!" I shout at the top of my voice, pushing him against the sink and off of me.
Within seconds, Dean is in the room rescuing me like I hoped he would. Stupid me assuming this really, considering I've never gone this far and backed down before, but I'm glad he did storm in.

"Dean, I will see you tomorrow. Thank you" I whisper, whilst he holds the man back, who is now attacking me with insulting words.

7:59am (Thursday 25th March)

"Morning girls, how was your night?" Mr Harper

chirps, walking into the building in the morning.

Sitting behind our desk we tell him it went well, but we're clearly both lost deep in thought.

"And how's the mouth, Christina?" he asks me.

Mouth? Mouth? What's he talking about?

"Excuse me?" I respond, as Jenna kicks me underneath the desk for some... "Oh the tooth? The dentist? Yeah, all is fine" I tell him, claiming it's been a long and exciting night, especially with the Jentina nightclub sign in my view all this time.

"Jenna showed you inside then, did she?" he asks, before asking whether I liked it.

"Liked it? I loved it" I assure him, claiming the naming of the place touched me so much, that I've actually been spaced out all night long.

Obviously I know why I'm feeling out of it this morning, but I can hardly tell Mr Harper this, can I? It's all the Jenna and Greg stuff – It's all me pulling away from another man – It's all me being... Oh, I have no idea how I'm feeling right now, but one thing is for sure – Jenna isn't the person I always thought she was.

"When you girls get into work tonight, the hotel will be complete" Mr Harper tells us, as we ready to leave.

I thought it was complete. Isn't it? Is it? Wow, I need to go home and sleep.

"Girls" he calls out, as we head for the exit. "Loving the new uniform by the way" he adds, with a huge smile on his face.

Uniform? What uniform? Aren't I naked then? Jenna was completely naked last night, wasn't she?

All I can do is smile, wave and leave, knowing a good regrouping and my head sorting out is needed before coming back into work tonight.

CHAPTER 4 – *SECRET PASSAGE*

It's like one extreme to the next with me, isn't it? Yesterday I slept in and was really late for work, then today I'm up at three in the afternoon, unable to sleep. Wow, I can't believe how much information is flooding my head right now. I still can't believe I've been promoted - I still can't believe the hotel looks so amazing - I still can't believe now coming into day four, I haven't had any sex whatsoever – Yet most of all, I still can't get my head around just how sexual Jenna was last night. Seriously, think about someone you've known for ages, who hasn't mentioned anything sexual in all that time, then you should know how I feel. Then take that person and watch them go sexually insane for just one night and that's what I'm dealing with today!

As I get out of bed to have something to eat early, realizing I can relax and take my time today, still Jenna is flooding my mind. The things I heard coming out of her mouth - The things I saw her do - And let's not forget her blatant nakedness in front of me. Up until yesterday, I'd watched her dress like a nun for almost twelve months, yet she hardly left anything to the imagination, did she? How can I eat, when all I can vision in front of me is her little brown pubic hair area? Damn it, I will get ready for work instead, then pick up something to eat on the way in for a change.

Oh no, I forgot about this, didn't I? The new dreaded uniform, where me wearing a skirt is no longer required. How am I supposed to feel sexy in a pair of trousers? Oh well, time to have a shower, take them through with me and hopefully make them sit on my body and look hot before I leave.

God damn it, this shower is no good either, because I just can't stop my mind from ticking. If I'm totally honest with myself, none of this has got anything to do with Jenna, because it's really all about me. Me, who didn't think before acting in that room with Greg – Me not seeing it all sooner, when he clearly wasn't interested – Then me, sliding down on top of his body, doing something I now regret. See, it doesn't matter how hot or horny I feel, I'd never stoop so low as to sleep with a friends man and although I wouldn't exactly call Jenna a real friend, I still feel guilty as hell about it. Oh how my job and new career could be crushed, if Jenna ever found out – Seriously, it's not even worth thinking about!

Okay, I'm showered, I'm clean, so let's do something with this uniform, shall we? Wow, all this thinking about Greg is making me feel really horny again. So hot in-fact, that I'm considering dropping this towel, heading back to bed and doing something about it now I have plenty of time on my hands. Note to self – On my next pay day, get online and purchase yourself a huge sex toy or something. Anything to reach the spots you're currently feeling, where fingers just won't do it.

Once again, now it's on, I do really like this new blouse. With the right bra on; like I have on right now, my cleavage looks perfect. Okay, now for these trousers. A nice black pair of knickers already on today, because those tatty old purple ones yesterday were a crime to wear and it's up with these trousers I go. No, not liking the feel of them, and not liking the look of them in the mirror either.

"Okay, plan B" I sigh to myself, knowing there's only one thing for it.

As I pull the uncomfortable and unforgiving trousers off, I quickly take off my knickers in a bid to go commando today. I then put the trousers back on, check out my ass in the mirror and feel much better about it.

"Round, not too big, not too small. Yeah, that will get me some overdue attention today" I sing to myself, finally ready to leave for work early.

After I've had something to eat, then traveled to work on the train, teasing different men with my new tight camel-toe look trousers, I arrive outside the building almost two hours early for work at six. I stand admiring the outside for a couple of minutes, then head inside to a vision I've never seen before. Not only is Mr

Harper clearly hard at work again, not only is Jentina's music being pumped out of the open door to entertain him, but there are another six or seven male builders racing around the building, all seemingly trying to get finished off in time. Look at that, the old metal staircase is even being replaced by two of the men as I arrive. Wow, that new wooden staircase is so much warmer and less prison looking, isn't it?

A "*What the hell are you doing here*" is what I expect to receive when Mr Harper notices me standing in reception, but instead I get another version of it instead.

"Christina, grab that kitchen cupboard over there and take it through to the guys in the dining room" Mr Harper calls out, doing something beside the wall.

A hello would have been nice. Saying that, noticing me being a petite female would have been nice too, seeing as there's no way I should be lifting something this heavy.

"Oh and Christina" he calls out, as I start to grapple with the kitchen furniture. "Hello" he adds with a smile. Seriously... How does this guy always seem to be able to read my mind, or say the right thing at the right time?

I respond with a smile back, then lift the heavy kitchen cupboard up in my arms. No sooner have I walked two steps with it, when a big, strong looking workman immediately takes it from me with a "*Let me help you with that*" smile. Be my guest I think to myself, instantly smiling back at him, then strangely feeling stupid watching him carry it with ease. Cor, look at his ass, whilst he carries it. Is it just me, or have I just realized I'm in a hotel alone with a load of men? Surely one of these guys aren't married? Surely one would like to take a break and spend some time with...

"Sorry Mr Harper, what was that?" I call out, realizing I'm not listening as usual.

"What brings you into work so early today?" he says, as he hangs a few nice pictures on the wall in reception.

"I couldn't sleep, so I thought I'd come in and offer some help" I tell him, knowing the first part of my statement is true anyway.

As Mr Harper looks around for things I can help with, yet struggles to spot anything, it's here where I do finally realize I'm of no use to anyone.

"You could go and stock the bar in Jentina, if you like?" he finally calls out.

Oh, maybe I was wrong, maybe I can be of some assistance after all. Wow, I wonder if there's a hot guy working in there at the moment? You know, to give me something to look at, whilst I kindly offer to start my shift here early?

7:45pm (Thursday 25th March)

"Once Jenna has turned up, I will give you the final tour of the place, but I think you can already tell the place is just about finished" Mr Harper tells me, coming into Jentina an hour later, when I've just stocked the bar to perfection.

There's a question I need to ask, isn't there? Come on Christina, get it out whilst he's talking to you, otherwise you will forget it, just like you forgot to tell him about... Oh yeah...

"Mr Harper, I know it's not my place to say, but I think the new rooms could do with a mirror in them" I quickly announce, remembering my encounter in the room yesterday, which lead me into the bathroom to find Greg.

"Good idea Christina. Come and show me where" he instantly responds, claiming these ideas are what he's hiring his manageress for, so pleased that I'm taking an interest.

As I follow him towards room number two downstairs and he uses his key-card to open the door, I ready myself to announce where I think the mirror in the bedroom should go.

"Right over there, where you have already placed a mirror" I tell him, noticing a huge mirror on the wall, which makes me feel a little silly.

"Great minds think alike, Christina" he chirps in my direction, before asking if I've got any more great ideas.

As I look around the finished room, struggling to find anything else wrong with it, I do happen to notice the little glory hole still sitting in the wall.

"You could fill that hole in over there" I tell him, obviously being funny.

"Yeah, that was supposed to be done today, but the control pads haven't turned up" he explains. "Until the rooms are properly functional, we won't be charging full price to our guests" he adds.

TV's not working, control pads not turned up yet, lower the price for the rooms, got it!

Although I spend the next ten minutes making myself look pretty, or at least busy knowing I'm really not helping at all, I watch as all the workmen finish their duties and even manage to pick out the one I like the look of most.

8:07pm (Thursday 25th March)

"Have you got any idea where Jenna is tonight?" Mr Harper asks, as I take my position at the reception desk, knowing my shift has now started.

"No Mr Harper, I haven't got a clue" I tell him, instantly feeling bad about this.

Yesterday when I was late, Jenna obviously covered for me and said I was at the dentist. Yet if I was to cover for her, surely I would have done that when I walked in at six and not past the time of her arrival, as I wonder where she is myself?

"Oh well, I guess she's got good reason. Tell her about the lowering of the prices for the next few days and good luck now all eight rooms are functional" he tells me, ready to leave and go home.

As I watch an exhausted Mr Harper and the final workman leave, the first thought to come to mind is – Wow, I hope one has stayed behind and wants some sex with me. Quickly, I dismiss this thought when I realize I'm alone, then panic a little that I might have to take care of up to eight rooms by myself tonight, if Jenna doesn't turn up.

8:42pm (Thursday 25th March)

Finally, here she comes some forty-two minutes late... No, maybe not, because this couple walking in right now don't appear to look like her.

"Welcome to the Cure Hotel, can I help you?" I sing out in my professional manageress voice, as the couple approach me at the desk.

On first impression, these two look fine. They are smartly dressed and both have a huge smile on their faces.

"We need a room for the night" the man in his forties says, clutching the female he's with tightly.

Fair enough, but now you've got a lot closer, I can actually see she's a lot younger than you. In-fact, she looks like someone around my age, so surely she can't be your wife.

"We've got an important meeting tomorrow morning here in town, so my assistant and I need to do a lot of work tonight and don't need to be disturbed" he tells me.

Did I say anything? Was I going to disturb you? MM-mm, very suspicious, because that skirt she's wearing or the way you're looking at her right now, wouldn't suggest you're going to be getting much work done. Hey, who am I to judge? If he had of turned up on his own, even with that wedding band around his finger, I still might have tried it on with him.

"That will be forty dollars for the night, Sir" I tell him, punching their details into my new computer. "Unfortunately, the TV's aren't wired up to our new control pad system yet, but our new nightclub Jentina is open for business" I add.

Listen to me proudly promote the hell out of my new night-spot already.

"I don't think we will have time for dancing, thank you very much" he answers abruptly, as I instantly notice the girl beside him frown.

Yeah, I guess you will end up having no time to work either by morning, because she's so your assistant here for a little fling, isn't she?

"And what's the name, please?" I ask, knowing this is the part of my job, where I find out if they're married or not.

"I'm Timothy Smith and this is Lara Ditcot" he answers.

Knew it, I knew you two weren't married and this night is nothing but a... Hold on, he already told me they were colleagues, didn't he? So why am I getting all suspicious? Wow Christina, you've really got to start listening more, because...

"Sorry Sir, what was that?" I then crazily ask, not listening again.

"Our names or records of this booking aren't disclosed or shared online, are they?" he asks.

I don't know what kind of hotel you've been staying in before now Sir, but this is the Cure Hotel. Oh I see, you don't want anyone to find out you've been here, do you?

"No Sir, what happens at the Cure Hotel, stays at the Cure Hotel" I quickly respond, giving him a little playful wink.

"Are you trying to imply something, young Lady?" he grunts at me. "Do you value your job?" he asks, seemingly upset with me now.

What did I do? I only announced his stay would be at the height of my discretion and...

"There's nothing going on between my assistant and I. We're here to work, okay?" he growls again, before I've had a chance to respond.

Oh I see, you're a lying bastard as well, are you Sir? Although you're telling me your seedy visit must be totally discrete, you're trying to make me believe it's innocent as well, are you? Fair enough, I can play dumb – Perhaps pretend to be your wife, considering she must be really thick letting someone like you out of her sight!

"Enjoy your evening" I say politely enough, handing

him the key-card for room number one, keeping all my thoughts and insults to myself.

I hope she gives you Thrush, you...

"Oh and when I call for room service later" he calls out, heading towards their room. "There's going to be someone at the desk, isn't there?" he asks.

"Of course Sir" I respond, calling him a pompous twat under my breath.

"Where the hell are you letting them go?" growls Jenna, suddenly entering the building, pointing at the couple going into their room.

Wow, what's with everyone's attitude tonight?

"Room one" I announce, slightly confused by the question, but pleased to see her turn up for work at least.

"A room Mr Harper has told us not to use, until he says so?" she huffs, reaching the desk.

Oh that's right, you don't know we're fully open now, do you Jenna? No, you're just turning up an hour late for work, missing all Mr Harper told me, aren't you? I mean, it's not like you didn't enjoy that room yourself all last night and...

"Well?" she growls again, clearly waiting for my answer.

Once I've explained what Mr Harper told me when I arrived early today, she seems to back down quick enough, but then attacks me again.

"So, did you cover for me?" she asks.

"I... I... I couldn't, because I got here at six" I try to explain, hoping she understands the dilemma I found myself in earlier.

"Thanks very much" she huffs, giving me a really dirty look, before heading off somewhere.

"Jenna, is everything okay?" I call out, feeling slightly

bad about not covering for her.

"I'm going for an early break" she tells me, strangely heading into the secret passageway door, obviously because she can't stand to be around me already tonight. Should I tell her she's only just walked into work? No, bad idea Christina, considering you're already in her bad books and this would surely make her even more furious at you.

9:32pm (Thursday 25th March)

"Good evening Mr Hodge" I sing out, watching him drag himself into our new hotel, quickly realizing his horrifying face doesn't fit here any longer.

"R... room three, p... please, Christina" he stutters, reaching the desk.

"That will be one hundred dollars, please Mr Hodge" I announce, hoping the high price will put him off.
Yes I do realize I'm not sticking to what Mr Harper told me about the price of rooms until the control pads are fixed, but this is Mr Hodge. I don't want to give him a room on the cheap, so he can tarnish the new look with his creepy presence, then expect the same price forever more.

"I... I... I will g... give you sixty dollars" he says.
I'm not sure which hotel Mr Hodge has stayed in before, considering he almost lives here anyway, but I don't think haggling or... Oh great and here comes Gary Sheen now.

"Don't tell anyone Mr Hodge, but I will give you the room for sixty dollars tonight as a special treat" I quickly whisper, needing him out of the way quickly, because I can't deal with him and Gary at the desk at the same time.

"I... I... knew you... you liked m... me really Christina" he grumbles, with a freaky smile on his face.

Oh no, err, no, it's err, it's not like that Mr Hodge, I was just being... Oh damn it...

"Evening Mr Sheen, what can I do for you?" I sing out, watching Mr Hodge drag himself towards room three, knowing if Gary is staying too, then he's going to have to accept room two now, not his usual number one room.

"Has that grumpy cow Jenna still got me on the black list?" he quickly whispers, looking around as though she might jump out on him.

You know what? I agree, she is a grumpy cow.

"Room for two, Gary?" I quickly ask, knowing I have to get him in, locked away and settled before Jenna returns from the sulking room beyond.

"Unless you want to check in with me as well" he chirps, in his usual charming womanizing manner.

Cor, on a normal night feeling the way I do, I think I would right now, but seeing as I'm just pissing everyone off tonight, I'd better keep my legs crossed for a little while longer.

Once Gary has taken the key-card for room two then attempted to touch my bum, changing his mind because I have these disgusting trousers on, I'm at least happy that he was willing to pay full price and not haggle me down like Mr Hodge did.

11:21pm (Thursday 25ᵗʰ March)

I haven't got any idea where Jenna disappeared to when she walked in tonight and I haven't seen her since. She's either sulking or sleeping out back somewhere, so I decided to leave her to it, considering I've got to get used to doing this night shift thing alone soon enough anyway. I welcomed Gary's lady friend in for the night - I reluctantly completed Mr Hodge's creepy coke run request - I watched Mr Smith race in and out of the hotel twice; obviously talking to his wife on the phone - Then I checked Gary and his ruffled female friend out again ten minutes ago.

It's been a busy night without Jenna beside me, but at least I haven't had to put up with her moaning. Wow, we've got to get us some better guests soon. I mean, what's the point in my lovely Jentina nightclub, if Gary only comes in for a quickie, Mr Hodge just acts weird all night long, then the other couple don't even venture out of their room? I want a packed hotel with younger people – People that want me to lock the front door, then dance and party all...

"Sorry Jenna, what was that?" I suddenly ask, not even noticing her turn up at the desk beside me, whilst deep in thought about the future of this hotel.

"I said you can go for your break now" she grunts.

"But it's only half eleven. I don't usually take my..."

"Take it now, Christina. Take it now!" she cuts me off, giving me a death glare, then ushers me towards the main door.

MM-mm, I've got a bad feeling about this. Why did a cold shiver just race up my spine, then make me feel that her stupid boyfriend Greg has said something to her about the other night? Okay Christina, it's only a thought, so just go on your break. Don't question it, don't ask anything, because she could just be in a foul mood like she's usually in every few days.

11:32pm (Thursday 25ᵗʰ March)

Okay, slightly earlier than I wanted to head over to Dean's bar, but let's do this. A man is what I need and a man is what I'm going to receive tonight, even if it's Dean himself.

Oh shit... What's going on now? Why is the bar closed yet again? Ooh, no wait, Dean is inside and now coming over to the door.

"What do you want Christina?" he grumps at me.
What's with everyone tonight? Has everyone taken the same "*Hate Christina*" pill or something?

"A drink, some sex, not necessarily in that order" I tell him, trying to lighten the mood, as he swings the door open to let me inside.

"Jump up on the bar, open your legs, because a fuck is something I can do" he sings out, clearly not joking like I am, but at least talking to me. "Drink? Why bother have me serve you one? Haven't you got enough of that across the street now?" he asks, with a touch of sarcasm in his voice.

Oh I see, you've heard about Jentina, have you? But how?

"I was informed today that a local premises had been approved an all night liquor license, then was shocked to find out it was you guys" he explains, showing me exactly why he's upset with me, which is more than Jenna has done tonight.

Does Dean actually know I don't own the hotel? I mean, does he know it was Mr Harper that would have applied for it and not me?

Once Dean has explained that his business has been crumbling lately and our hotel might be the final nail in his coffin, I feel a little responsible. Obviously not too responsible, seeing as it would be happening whether I was employed at the Cure or not, but bad nevertheless. Quickly I come up with an idea that might be a good one, depending on how he takes it. I tell him to pour me a drink, then I sit at the bar telling him I've got something to say.

"In a few weeks time, I'm going to become night manageress over at the hotel" I tell him.

"Well, I'm really pleased for you, Christina" he quickly responds, not letting me finish.

"I'm going to be allowed to hire three employees to work with me" I then tell him.

Okay, now he's not saying anything, which is a little concerning. No, no it isn't – He just doesn't know what I'm talking about now, so carry on.

"Why don't you come and work for me?" I ask him, cutting to the confusing chase.

The silence in Dean's empty bar falls even more silent, as I worry that he's going to be offended by my offer. Then he finally has something to say, whilst I start to enjoy my drink...

"I own this place Christina, I am my own boss. What makes you feel I would be any better off with you being my manager?" he asks, clearly not impressed by my offer then.

I quickly tell him that the job with me; obviously if Mr Harper lets me hire a barman, is hassle free from running his own business and trying to keep it afloat. I then tell him that Mr Harper; who will become his real boss, pays really well. Then finally I tell him that I will be over there with him, so we have plenty of...

"Okay, I will do it!" he suddenly chirps.

"Really?" I question, feeling my sales woman pitch was a little bit flat myself.

"Sell my business, have a little cash in my back pocket, then work with you. Why not? It sounds fun" he responds, pouring me another drink to celebrate.

Okay, at what part of this offer was it already a done deal? Surely he knows I'm going to have to run it past my own boss and see what...

"I'm going to open this place for the next couple of days and sell all my stock at half price" he beams as though I've lifted a huge weight off his shoulders. MM-mm, and I'm going to have to talk to Mr Harper in the morning and pray he likes this idea too, otherwise you will really have reason to be upset with me.

Although I came over here tonight to firstly get laid, then earlier than usual because Jenna's in such a bad mood, I find myself ready to head back to the hotel after just twenty minutes, because there's not much else to say. Yes, Dean is happy enough with me and shows this by racing around the bar to hug me, but it's hardly reason to have sex with him, is it? Or is it? I am feeling kind of frisky at the moment – four or five days celibate in my world, does strange things to a girl, you know. No, I can't, I'm now far too worried about talking to Mr Harper in the morning, then sorting out Jenna's problem, aren't I? Fuck this professional manageress lark, because it's destroying my sex life completely now!

12:03 am (Friday 26ᵗʰ March)

As the lonely walk back across the street to the hotel
takes a lot longer than it usually does, I start rehearsing
my speech to Mr Harper in the morning, then try to
figure out a way of sorting things out with Jenna too. I
head back inside the hotel, planning to just come out
with it and ask her what the problem is, but when I reach
reception, there seems to be a slight problem...

"Now where has she gone?" I question myself,
because she's simply not anywhere to be seen.
And I doubt myself being a manageress, because Jenna is
clearly more qualified than me – Yeah right, at least I
wouldn't ever leave reception unguarded. I mean,
anyone could walk in right now and take our computer.

I walk half way up the new stairs, so that I can see along
the landing corridor, but she's not there - I take a look
over the banister at the ground floor, but Jenna's
nowhere to be seen - I then head back downstairs and
take a quick look inside Jentina, but again no sign of my
illusive colleague.

"I know where she is" I chirp to myself, heading
towards the downstairs secret passage door.
I've never been in here before, but I guess with this new
access-all-areas key-card Mr Harper left me today, I will
be able to open this door at last. MM-mm, just as I
thought, it works. Come on then Jenna, what do you do
hiding in here all the time? Secret TV? Vodka bottle
stashed in here with you? Or is this where Greg stays
most nights?

Wow, isn't this passageway narrow? I mean, there's a

wall, there's me in the middle, then there's another wall, with wires hanging everywhere. Oh, this must be the walkway behind all the downstairs rooms and look, the little glory holes from the other side of those walls too. Let's have a little peek, shall we? No Christina, bad Christina, you're the manageress, not a pervert. Oh bugger it – Like there's anything that could keep my wandering eye away from it now I'm so desperate to see what's inside. Wow, look at the hotel room from this angle. Seriously, if anyone was in the room right now, I'd so be able to spy on them. Okay, this must be room four, because there's nobody inside it. The next hole I'm coming to, must be room three, which I ain't going to look through either, because Mr Hodge is in there. MM-mm yeah, let's have a look into Gary Sheen's room, shall we? My god, if anyone caught me doing this right now, I'd definitely get fired or arrested for sure!

"Okay Gary, cover it up, I'm about to have a look" I whisper to myself, not sure what I'm hoping to find, but knowing he's in there with a prostitute anyway.

Or maybe not... No, just an empty messy bed, because I've just realized through my weird craziness, that I already checked Gary out of the hotel tonight, didn't I? Fair enough, I'm going crazy, but at least around this corner should be the hole for room number one, where I know Mr Smith and his young assistant Lara Didcot haven't checked out yet. Yeah, let's see if you are doing the work you claimed you needed to be doing tonight, and whether or not you're just...

"WHAT THE FUCK?..."

Wow, I'm glad I didn't just say that out loud, quickly hide Christina!

As I recompose myself behind the wall; to the corner I almost turned then, I take a quick peek round it to find what I thought I saw, when I nearly walked straight into this dilemma. Okay, this is getting weird now. Two days ago I thought Jenna was a prudish virgin – Yesterday, I found out she enjoyed sex as much as me – And now tonight, I stand here behind this wall, almost bumping into her with her eye glued against the hole of room one, her trousers around her ankles and her hand apparently inside her knickers. I mean, this is incredible! No, it's err, it's insane. In-fact, I don't actually know if this is right now. Look at the way she's masturbating – Look at the way she's going for it – My god, what is she seeing through the hole that is making her feel so hot? Fucking hell, just imagine her mood, if she caught me watching her, watching them right now.

As soon as I fear it, I find myself scampering back to the exit, needing to be out in the reception area again fast.

12:11 am (Friday 26th March)

This is mental. Why am I sitting back at the reception desk trembling? I haven't done anything wrong. Wow, I just can't shake the image of her watching them like that out of my head. Maybe I should go and knock on room number ones door and stop them doing whatever it is they are doing inside? No, how would I stand in their room and not be able to take my own eyes away from Jenna's eyeball at the hole in the wall at the other side? She'd surely realize I then know she's doing whatever it is she is doing? Okay Christina, calm down, take a deep breath and think. It's not that bad – I have sex with

95

guests in those rooms, Jenna likes to watch, there's nothing wrong with it. Although now saying that, yes there is, because surely what she's doing is against the law without consent. Okay, Okay, walk yourself over to Jentina, maybe another little drink will take the edge off it all.

No sooner have I reached the bar and I'm already pouring myself a second drink to calm my nerves, because I swallowed the whole first glass without noticing. This is huge – This is massive – This is... I haven't got a clue!

"Okay, no more drink" I tell myself five minutes later. "Go out there and do your job" I whisper to myself, claiming I haven't done anything wrong, if wrong isn't spying on masturbating Jenna, spying on others?

I pick up my empty glass, planning to wash it in the dining room kitchen; so I'm not caught drinking on duty, then strangely exit Jentina and creep towards the dining room door, as though I have done something wrong.

"What's wrong with you Christina? Stop creeping around, there's nothing to worry about and there's..."

Oh no, spoke too soon, didn't I? What is this on the floor, outside the dining room, if it isn't a blood stain? No, it's a little more than a blood stain, because it's more like a puddle of blood on the floor, as I take a closer look. Okay, think, think, keep thinking, not that you've actually thought anything since discovering Jenna's secret jerk-off vantage point.

As I enter the dining room, it's then I realize this room has only been finished today. I thought the guys in here earlier were starting to build the kitchen out back, but it seems to be finished just like the rest of the hotel. Okay, take your empty glass into the kitchen, rinse it out quickly, splash some water over your face and get with...

"HOLY SHIT, MOTHER OF.... WOW, Jenna, you scared the life out of me" I scream, walking into the kitchen to find my masturbating colleague at the sink, clearly washing her sticky fingers, not masturbating any longer.

"What the hell are you screaming at Christina? Can't you see I've hurt myself?" she grunts, showing me her finger is badly cut.

Oh, that would explain the blood on the floor then, wouldn't it?

"What happened?" I ask, shaking everything off, then trying to sound concerned for her, whilst my heart beats louder than the whole building.

"Someone didn't hammer a nail in properly and I caught my finger on it" she informs me, instantly blaming a workman and his shoddy craftsmanship.

"What nail, where?" I ask, instantly wanting her to show me it's a nail in the secret passageway, so I can randomly spot the holes in the wall, then maybe point them out for a reaction.

"Did I say nail? I meant a knife" she then says, pointing over to a really sharp knife on the counter, which does clearly have traces of blood on it.

How would you walk into and catch your finger on a knife? Saying that, what were you doing in... Oh it doesn't matter, I think cleaning her up should be my only priority right now.

2:16am (Friday 26th March)

Jenna and I have been sitting in reception not doing

much for the last hour and a half. Yes, her finger has stopped bleeding and yes we cleaned the blood off the floor. Since then, nothing! She's clearly not in a chatty mood on this shift - I've clearly got one question I want to ask her - But all I keep thinking about is my discovery and how is she going to masturbate tomorrow, whilst her fingering finger is wrapped up? Seriously, this hotel can and will drive me totally insane one day, because it's all so very boring on nights like this, yet so much random stuff floods your head and... Ooh action, someone is emerging from room number one. They've probably spotted the hole in the wall and want to question us about it.

"Hello Miss Didcot, how can I help you?" I sing out, knowing I remember her name and Jenna won't, so that's a good manageress point awarded to me.

Not that her watching these guests and masturbating shouldn't be an instant ten point deduction!

"Yeah, you haven't seen Timothy Smith, my boss around here, have you?" she asks.

As I strangely take a look around our huge empty reception area, then think I might have spotted him, but it's only one of the new huge plants, I tell her no.

"I did see him earlier at around eleven, rushing in and out of the hotel with his phone" I tell her.

"Yeah, that's when he was on the phone to his wife" she declares.

"Then maybe he's gone back home to his wife" Jenna suddenly barks, giving her a dirty disproving look, then offering to have a look outside in the street for him.

"Don't worry about her" I playfully joke, as stroppy Jenna walks towards the main door. "She cut her finger earlier and has been moaning about it ever since" I add.

7:48am (Friday 26th March)

All in all it's been quite a crazy night, but Jenna's mood and masturbating skills have no doubt shocked me the most. Wow, I hope she's in a better mood tonight, now it's Friday. One more shift, then I have the weekend off and boy do I need it right now!

"Morning girls, did you enjoy your night?" sings Mr Harper, walking over to the desk, bright eyed and bushy tailed this morning.

"No!" grunts Jenna.

I think this is the moment where we tell Mr Harper we did have a wonderful night, even if we didn't, Jenna.

"No? Oh why, what happened?" responds Mr Harper, sounding genuinely concerned.

"One of your workmen friends left a nail out of place and I cut my finger quite badly on it" she growls at him.

I thought it was Professor Plum that did it, with a knife, in the dining... Oh you're off home, are you Jenna? See you later then. That's right, don't say goodbye, I haven't just put up with your bad mood all night long, have I?

"Is she okay?" Mr Harper asks me, as though I know anything.

"I think so" I respond, giving off a nervous chuckle and a hint of shrugged shoulders in the process too.

Once I've told Mr Harper who's staying in the hotel and who he will be checking out this morning, he's slightly disappointed that only three of the rooms were used last night. Although it's not the best of times, I then decide to go for it and ask the question I've been waiting to ask him all night long...

"When I get to hire these three employees, would it be

okay if I hired myself a barman for Jentina?" I ask.

Waiting for him to say no, or at least dance around the question a little bit first, he sets me straight immediately.

"The three staff members you hire Christina, are people of your own choice" he tells me. "The kitchen and bar will have staff already, that won't impact who you employ" he adds.

Bugger... That means he's going to hire the barman himself, doesn't it?

"It's just the bar across the street is closing down in a few days time, so I thought you might want to..."

"What's his name Christina, and can you vouch for him?" Mr Harper cuts me off, ironically cutting to the chase.

"Dean is a great barman and a very good friend of mine" I tell him, instantly vouching for the friendly barman.

"Then if he wants the job, it's his" he responds, with a smile.

Wow, that was a lot easier than I thought it was going to be. Why can't Jenna be more like Mr Harper? Great, now I can go over to the bar and tell him later on tonight. Maybe even get myself a man in the process, because I don't think this sexual frustration thing is doing me any favors, especially when Jenna seems to be doing whatever she wants to do these days. Wow, how the tides have changed since Mr Harper took over!

CHAPTER 5 - *PERFORMANCE*

Have I slept much today? Have I hell. It's five o'clock in the evening, I've showered, eaten and I'm dressed ready for work, tempting myself to turn into a real life zombie. Seriously, it's as though I understand so much I've never understood before now. I used to hear people claim how stressful their jobs were, but never believed any job was worth stressing out about. Since I've been promoted however, I no longer feel like a nineteen year old girl and I'm sure Jenna's crazy antics have given me my first gray hair.

Today is the day I'm going to sort everything out. Never will I put up with Jenna's bad mood again and never will I let her boss me around. Although I don't believe in blackmail, I now know what she gets up to of an evening when she disappears, so I'm pretty much going to hold this against her. Okay maybe not, seeing as I'm too much of a coward to go through with the whole blackmail part, but I am going to do something remarkable tonight. Yeah, I'm going to enjoy my Friday night, because I have two days off after this shift and if I don't get laid tonight, it's okay, because I will be going out at the weekend and having sex like a crazed nymphomaniac anyway. I will show Jenna she isn't as sexual as I am!

As I make my way to work, still the positive thoughts echo out in my mind. I have sex in those rooms, Jenna watches, so where's the harm? Yes, nothing has changed since I convinced myself it was illegal yesterday, but to be honest, I want to know what she's looking at. I mean, what if I'm missing out on something amazing myself? My plan tonight is simple... Question her about the hole watching thing as soon as I walk in, then on my break, have a quick look myself.

7:52pm (Friday 26ᵗʰ March)

"Good evening Christina. Did you have a nice rest?" chirps Mr Harper, as I walk into the hotel, to find Jenna already behind the desk beside him.

"Evening Christina. You ready for a great night?" chirps Jenna, with a huge smile on her face.
Damn it – That screws up my plan instantly, doesn't it? Wow, I was hoping she'd be in a bad mood tonight, so I could question and maybe blackmail her into being happy. Yet how can I do this, if she's happy already?

"How's the finger, Jenna?" I quickly ask, noticing the plaster covering up her injury this evening.

"It's fine, thanks Christina" she instantly responds. "In-fact, I've been using it on my vagina all afternoon" she then adds, blowing my mind.

Did she just say that in front of... Yes, she did, look at Mr Harper's face turn red and...

"And, I think that's my cue to leave you to it" he then blushes some more, heading for the door as soon as it's said.

Seriously, did she really just say that? Is she actually smiling at me? More importantly, is she turning into the old sexual me and I'm turning into a prudish version of her? Fucking hell, I feel another gray hair emerging from my roots and it's only the start of the night. What do I have to do to become me again? I'm the sexier one – I'm the sexual one – I'm the...

"Good evening Mr Sheen, room for one, or would you like me to join you tonight?" I then shockingly watch her greet the man she hated the last time they spoke.

"I don't know who your friend is Christina, but I like her style" he playfully responds my way, obviously knowing it's Jenna, before offering her a few hours with him.

"Christina, watch the desk" Jenna whispers, giving me a wink. "We're going to take room six upstairs, because we're already so busy tonight" she tells him, grabbing the key-card to that said room, before heading around to his side of the desk.

Am I dreaming this or something? Am I actually seeing this right? Has Jenna just appeared from this side of the desk, wearing our old uniform? More importantly, why isn't she wearing her usual black prudish tights with it? Wow, look at her legs, as the horny couple walk up the staircase together. Hold on... I'm the one needing to get laid tonight – I'm the one that's single. What about Greg? Have they split up or something? Wow, she's really doing this, isn't she? Have I really become the prude behind the desk, whilst Jenna turns into what I used to like being?

8:32pm (Friday 26th March)

It's been a whole half an hour since Jenna took Gary Sheen up to room number six and fuck do I feel even more sexually frustrated now. I can only sit here and imagine what they're doing together, knowing what it's like to be with a lover like Gary myself, whilst understanding what Jenna has to offer her male partners these days. Seriously, it's tormenting my mind so much, that I've almost willed myself to run upstairs, enter the secret passageway, then have a peek through the hole at them myself. If that's not bad enough, it's taken all this time to finally register what Jenna said when Gary arrived. She said this place was busy tonight, yet I can't imagine where all these new people have come from. As I look at the computer screen, I try to work it out...

Room 1: Mr and Mrs Grayden
I don't know this couple.

Room 2: Simon Hall
I Don't know him.

Room 3: Garth Taylor and David Lindsay
Neither do I know these guys.

Room 4: Mr Leon Singer and Miss Trudy Potts
No, I don't know this couple.

Room 5: Cecil Douglas

Who are these people?

Room 6: Gary Sheen
Okay yeah, I obviously know him.

Where's Bill Hodge? Surely she didn't turn him away tonight? No matter how much the old guy freaks me out, he's never actually done anything worth worrying about and... Oh dear, until now perhaps, because speak of the devil, here he comes. Wow, I hope if Mr Hodge does stay here tonight, he doesn't mind climbing the stairs to room seven, because we're apparently full on the ground floor?

"Good evening Mr Hodge, room for one, is it?" I greet him at the reception desk, like I always do.

"No t... thank you C... Christina. I was in e... earlier and J... Jenna asked me to p... p... pay forty dollars" he grumbles at me.

"Well, that is the going rate Mr Hodge. That's until our rooms are completely func..."
Damn, I charged him sixty dollars last night, didn't I? No wonder he's looking at me like that. Think Christina, think...

"There you go Mr Hodge. I apparently over charged you by twenty dollars last night, so here's a refund" I offer him it quickly, so he doesn't try to murder me with his stare, then chop my body up using his smile.

"T... t... thank you Christina" he stutters, taking the money from me, which I have secretly paid for out of my own pocket. "N... now a w... word of warning" he utters.
Oh great and now comes the warning. Didn't I just put things right by offering him his money back? Is he really going to tell me off for it as well? Do I need...

"Be... be... beware the quiet ones C... Christina" he

says, in his creepy voice. "W... watching may be... become more sin... sin... sinister, if you c... cover it up" he adds.
Is that it? Is that your warning? Okay then Mr Hodge, thanks for that.

"Would you like a room tonight?" I ask, trying to smile through the head fuck and the scare he's currently offering me.

"No!" he snaps.
Wow, why did that response just remind me of that nightmare I had about him a few days ago?

"So, you're not staying with us tonight then?" I ask again, trying to shake off the horrible feeling rattling through my body.

"No!" he snaps again.
Fucking hell Christina, give him something to say yes to, considering his unfriendly no is so tormenting.

"Have you got somewhere else to stay tonight then?" I ask, obviously knowing he has, otherwise he would be checking in by now.

"NO!" he yells, freaking me out completely, before turning and heading for the exit. "Be... beware Christina. B... b... bad things are h... happening in this hotel" he adds.
Is that right at this minute, or happened already? Or does he mean, they are going to happen? God damn it – Why does he always leave me hanging like this? Maybe it's Jenna, maybe she's in-fact a complete and utter mental case. After all, I didn't find out she was highly sexed until only the other day, did I? Wow, what if my so-called colleague is up in room six murdering Gary Sheen as I sit here? She's certainly got a mysterious side to her, that I didn't know about? MM-mm, maybe I should go and take a look through one of those holes after all. How the hell has this reception area got eerily darker all of a sudden?

Why if there are six rooms occupied, can't I hear a...

"WHAT THE FUCK!..." I scream, leaping out of my skin completely.

"Wow, I've never been welcomed to a hotel like that before" says some random guy, claiming he's been standing at the other side of the desk for a few minutes now.

"I'm... I'm sorry Sir, you.... you startled me. How can I help you?" I shake, shudder and stutter all at once, waiting for my heart to land back inside my body.

"That's okay Beautiful, it was my fault" he responds, with a huge sexy grin on his face.

Tall man, dark hair, fit looking body...

"Can I have a room, please?" he asks.

Husky voice, gorgeous eyes. Sure thing Stud, you can definitely have a room here...

"What's the name, please?" I ask, realizing my sanity has gone, my professionalism has gone too, yet if I do this correctly, it will all then return and my knickers will be the only thing disappearing at the end of it.

Damn... Which knickers have I put on today, because I can't remember? Oh that's right, I haven't got any on, because commando looks better on my ass in these trousers, doesn't it?

"The name is Brad. Brad Noble" he tells me.

Am I supposed to type this information into the computer right now? Oh well, just give him the key-card to room seven, not forgetting to bend over for his benefit first.

"Ouch!" I then find myself squealing out, whacking my head off the desk in my attempt to do something sexy in front of him. "There you go Mr Noble, have a nice stay" I quickly grouch, handing him his key-card, as my head starts to throb.

"Don't you want paying for the room then?" he asks.

Paying? Paying for what? What's he asking me to do exactly? I don't... Oh, I see, yes I do.

"Yes Sir, of course. That will be forty dollars please" I announce, not only blushing with embarrassment, but sweating nervously a little too.

As he hands over his money and I almost give up on doing anything sexy with him now, he continues talking as I struggle to stay focused.

"What's that over there? What's Jentina?" he asks, pointing over towards the door.

What is it, err, it's a... Come on, think...

"It's a little nightclub with a bar, Sir" I finally tell him, after thinking about it for a few seconds, as though I haven't got a clue myself.

"Any chance of a drink right now then?" he asks.

Wow, you want a room for me, to take up my time and now a drink, do you? Not asking for much, are you, Sir?

"Yes, just walk right in and Dean will..."

No Dean won't, because he's not working here yet, is he?

"Err, walk right in and I will be there in a few minutes to serve you" I correct myself, hoping there's a new, better confident me about to emerge, instead of the wreck I've suddenly become.

Okay Christina, he's gone, so pull yourself together. He's clearly flirting with you, so this should be easy. Just be yourself and...

"HOLY SHIT!" I scream out again, leaping out of my seat this time.

"Sorry Christina, I didn't mean to scare you" giggles just had sex face, Jenna.

Didn't mean to scare me? Didn't mean to scare me? I almost wet... Okay, I'm scared now, because your hands are clearly covered in blood and the shit Mr Hodge just left me thinking about.

"What's that?" I quickly ask, knowing I don't want to hear the truth, if the truth is what I fear it to be.

"Oh this... Gary was doing me up against the wall and the paint on the wall in that room isn't dry yet" she answers, showing me just how she placed her hands up against the red wall, whilst he pleasured her from behind.

That does it, I need to get laid and that Brad Noble inside Jentina is waiting for me. No more scary thinking - No more acting like Jenna once did - Time to find the old Christina, who at this stage would be eating Mr Noble for breakfast!

"Is Gary Sheen coming down to check out of his room now then?" I quickly ask, still fearing his dead body might be up there.

"Yeah look, here he comes now" sings Jenna, claiming she will sign him out, if I want to go and do something else.

9:15pm (Friday 26ᵗʰ March)

Oh well, here goes nothing then. It's over to Jentina to get my freak on. Wow, how I wish I was wearing my skirt just like Jenna is doing right now. MM-mm, I wonder if she'd lend me hers? No, silly idea Christina, stop stalling and get your ass in there.

Deep breath as I ready to open the door – Stop acting so bloody nervous, because you've done this a million times before - Get in there and show him this is your place, your nightclub and he isn't getting out alive, until he's delivered at least four orgasms.

"Hi..." I quickly say, walking into Jentina, instantly losing my confidence, as though I'm an innocent sweet little girl.

"I poured myself a drink and got you one too" he calls back, waiting for me to actually enter the room, claiming he hopes I don't mind.

Why would I mind? It's not as though he wasn't thinking about... Oh that's right, this is my hotel, isn't it? And he's just rudely helped himself and...

"No, that's okay" I respond, not giving my brain enough time to catch up with my mouth.

No sooner have I nervously reached the bar, when he throws his drink down his throat and opens his mouth sexily once again.

"I find you incredibly attractive, Christina" he says, looking at my name badge. "Although I don't do this often, would you like to come up to my room?" he asks, as though his gaze already knows my answer.

MM-mm, can I have my drink first at least? No? You're getting ready to leave, are you? Oh and now I've not even answered, nodded my head and let myself take your hand.

As he walks me back towards the door and I'm nothing but a willing participant, I urge myself to show some confidence, but it's just not there. That bitch Jenna, must have stolen...

"MM-mm, very nice Christina. You make sure you give him hell" Jenna calls out as the door opens, then he laughs in her direction.

"Would you rather go upstairs with her?" I rudely whisper, not liking the fact she seems to have all of my confidence hidden behind that desk.

What's wrong with me? Now I'm insecure and jealous of my former prudish friend, am I?

"You would need a million of her to drag me away from one of you" he whispers at me, with that same sexy smile.

Cor, aren't you tall? Oh look, here we go again, heading towards the staircase, where I haven't realized we're on the move. This is definitely a first – A man taking the lead and not me forcing myself onto a guest for a change!

As he swipes his key-card in the door upstairs, I just about find a little bit of confidence, yet as soon as the door opens, I freeze and almost change my mind again. I don't know if it's Jenna downstairs in reception, looking up at us – I don't know if it's because the last time I was with a man, I needed Dean to chase him off – Or whether I've become the manageress of this hotel and I'm not the same girl any longer - Either way, now I'm in this room alone with him, I'm not sure I actually want sex, but I don't want this to...

"Let me undo those for you" I seductively whisper, falling to my knees in front of his huge bulge, realizing he was just about to undo them anyway.

I know exactly what's wrong with me now – It's those bloody holes in the wall, isn't it? I just can't have sex in front of them, knowing Jenna might be watching.

Knowing I can't possibly allow him to undress me now, or have sex with me for that matter, I take him out semi-hard and start performing oral sex on him. I know as soon as he's fully hard, he's going to pull me up and want to have sex with me, but I cannot let this happen. Instead, I've got to give him the best blow job I've ever given in my life and make him ejaculate quickly.

"MM-mm yeah, I like that" he groans, as I twist, turn and open my mouth as wide as I can, getting started. Suddenly I find myself watching his orgasmic face, looking at the thing I'm slurping on, then strangely watching the hole too. The minute that thing changes color or I see an eyeball, I'm going to freak and... No, no I'm not, because there she is – That's Jenna watching us right now, isn't it? Okay Jenna, you like to watch, so it's time to show you what I'm made of.

"Do you want to fuck me, Brad?" I growl at my new man friend, whilst jerking him off and taking a breather. "If you do, you're going to have to stop me from sucking on you first" I call out, so Jenna watching can hear my dirty talking skills too.

Although I know my dampening trousers want to come off, I continue to give him the blow job of his life, where crashing back against the wall is the best resistance he's got to offer me.

"Are you going to cum in my mouth?" I seductively groan, standing up onto my feet, then bending over right in front of Jenna's spy hole. "Would you like to place your fingers in between my thighs?" I tease, forcing him into a premature throb, as finally he's able to fight back a little. He opens my trousers at the front, almost ripping them. As he slides his hand down the back of my tight outfit, then parts my ass-cheeks with his thumb, I brace for the first fingering I've had in weeks.

"Oh my god, you feel so wet" he instantly groans, as I feel two of his fingers penetrate me to perfection.

"It's about to get a whole lot wetter" I announce loudly, because my oncoming orgasm is about to arrive too.

With that he starts to cum, so I pull him out of my mouth. Usually I swallow, but today it's different. If Jenna wants to watch, then I want her to see it fly towards her at the hole. I aim him away from me, I let it spurt everywhere, then I cum all over his fingers at the same time.

Okay, not the orgasm I actually wanted, but fuck that was really nice! Now to go and confront Jenna about her fascination of watching downstairs.

9:47pm (Friday 26ᵗʰ March)

I've got to say it, I'm so much better than that. Okay, so the blow job I just gave was obviously good enough for him, but on the whole, I usually go a lot further when I get to that stage. What I did find out about myself tonight was, I find it really hot somebody watching me. Yes, I'm usually turned on by a slight risk of getting caught, but tonight I really enjoyed performing in front of a secret watcher, even though I knew it was Jenna.

Oh well, here I go then, back down to reception. And look at that, surprise-surprise, Jenna is already sitting there behind the desk, making out she hasn't been anywhere. Wow, she must have been doing this watching thing a for a long time, not to get caught already?

Brad Noble was a true gentleman and is currently in his shower. He told me before I left that he'd be back for me another time, so I'm not too disheartened that I didn't get to have sex with him tonight. All in all, that was...

"Did you enjoy that then, you filthy slut?" giggles Jenna sitting behind the desk, obviously still wanting to be friendly.

Did she just call me a slut? Didn't she just entertain Gary Sheen before I left for Mr Noble's room? Am I the one wearing the skirt this evening?

"I guess so" I answer with a simple smile, before going for it. "Why? Did you enjoy watching us then?" I ask.

"Excuse me?" she fumes almost immediately.

"Did you enjoy watching us?" I ask, repeating my question, assuring her it's okay, because I didn't mind.

"I have no idea what you're talking about Christina" she barks at me.

Wow, she really does close down fast, doesn't she?

"I didn't mean anything..."

"Christina, be quiet. I have a headache" she grumbles.

"But I was..."

"Seriously Christina, I can't listen to your pathetic voice right now, so shut up" she barks again. "In-fact, I don't feel well, so why don't you just go for your break and leave me alone" she insists, doing the suggestion thing she does, where I don't ever get much of a say.

I try to be friendly and this is where it gets me. Fine, I'm off to give Dean the good news about his new job then. You sit here and sulk, Weirdo!

11:02pm (Friday 26ᵗʰ March)

I've just let Dean know that he's got a job at the hotel if he wants it and he was over the moon about it. His bar was packed tonight, but then again, it always is packed on a Friday night. I'm not sure if it was because the weekend is here, or because he is doing what he said he'd do and is selling drinks at half price, but it's certainly a packed house over there. Yes, tonight I can tell Dean would have had sex with me and so would a few of the other guys in his bar, but after my little thing with Mr Brad Noble, I don't think settling for anything other than him tonight, would actually get me off. Saying that, Jenna's latest outburst has put me off slightly too, considering she was really happy before I entertained the possible man of my dreams room. I mean, what happened? Didn't Gary Sheen scratch her sexual itch properly tonight? Was she jealous that I got Mr Noble instead of her? Is she feeling guilty, because she just clearly cheated on Greg? Or has she finally come to terms with the fact, it doesn't matter how hard she tries to become me, it's not going to be that easy? Oh well, time to face the music and try to find out why she went off at me again.

As I cross the street an hour after leaving grumpy Jenna at the desk, thoughts start appearing in my mind, like they never have before. Maybe she got rid of me, just to try it on with Brad herself. You know, I line him up with an oral appetizer, then she head in twenty minutes later with the main course. No, that can't be right – How can a man be interested, after he's just cum? MM-mm, maybe she did kill Gary Sheen after all?

"Bad Christina, silly Christina" I whisper to myself, telling myself off for tempting fate, yet it would explain why there's a police car sitting outside the hotel on my return.

As I enter the hotel slightly concerned, yet feeling the car outside is obviously parked there for another reason, I'm then shocked when I do find two officers talking to Jenna at our desk.

"Is everything okay?" I question, joining them.

Wow, it's as though I had to ask, simply to stop myself turning round and running out of the building. I wouldn't mind, but I haven't done anything to make me feel like running, but my legs are still going right now. How do the cops showing up always make you feel like you've done something wrong? Saying that, if Jenna has gone and killed Gary in some crazy sex act, I'm ready to blab on her, because I'm quite frankly getting sick of her mood swings now.

"Sorry, what was that?" I find myself asking, realizing as usual, my brain has turned my ears off at a vital point.

"These officers are looking for Mr Smith" Jenna tells me.

Who? Oh, you're being nice to me again, are you Jenna? Why, worried these guys might find your perverted spy holes, are you? Need a friend now, do you? Oh well, at least it's not Gary they're looking for. MM-mm, look at this guy beside me, with his huge batman style utility belt and gun – I wouldn't mind...

"Sorry, what was that?" I ask again, realizing I'm still doing it, I'm not paying full attention.

"Do you know Mr Smith?" the other officer questions me.

"No" I answer, instantly feeling I'm being put on trial for something I haven't done, yet Jenna might have.

"Do you remember him checking into this hotel yesterday?" he then asks.

Smith? Smith? Do I remember a...

"No" I answer again, pretty sure of my answer.

Suddenly, the good looking officer shows me a picture of this Timothy Smith guy and I quickly realize it's the arrogant married man from yesterday with his young assistant Lara. Yeah, it's all coming back to me now.

"Do you remember him now, Miss?" I'm asked again, once the picture has lit up my face.

"No" I answer, instantly waiting for them to handcuff me, knowing I'm lying, they can see my lie too, and even Jenna is giving me a funny suspicious look now.

What? Mr Smith made sure his visit was at my highest discretion, didn't he? What am I supposed to say, yeah he was with his assistant and blow his cover? What kind of good manageress would that make me then?

"This man has gone missing and hasn't been seen since yesterday. Because his wife had a GPS tracking device installed on his phone, she knows he came here" the officer then explains.

Oh well then, why didn't you say that before? If she knows he was here already, why am I covering for him?

I take a look at the picture of him again, as though it might jog my memory, then suddenly realize I do remember him now. Strange that!

"Sorry, with all the going's on in this hotel, it's hard to keep track of who is staying and who is not" I explain, confessing I do remember him now.

"Yeah, we had all of three guests stay here the other night" Jenna chirps up, landing me right in the middle of my own lie perfectly, the Bitch!

Why would she say that? Is she trying to get me arrested or something? Quick Christina, think - Say something that doesn't connect you with...

"Sorry, what was that?" I ask, knowing the officer said

something else, but I didn't hear what he said for the third time tonight.

"I said, do you remember who he was with last night?" he asks again, obviously getting fed up with me. Oh what the hell...

"He was with his personal assistant, Lara Didcot" I announce. "I remember him telling me they had an important meeting here in town the next day" I add, spilling my guts finally.

As the police officers look at each other, as though I'm lying again, it turns out they'd already questioned Miss Didcot today and she told them she hadn't seen him. Silly girl, fancy lying to the police like that.

As I finally feel I've done my bit to support the police and the wonderful job they do in our local community, although I've dropped Lara well and truly in it, my problem is with Jenna as the officers finally leave.

"Why did you make me look stupid like that?" I growl at her, the second they've gone. "For someone that clearly likes to watch, I would have thought you'd have told them everything about him anyway" I add, turning on my own bitchy style.

Okay, not the best way to tell her I'm okay with her perverted watching thing or breaking the ice about it, but I'm a little furious at her right now. Oh and now she's seemingly furious at me too. Why what did I do?

"Where are you going Jenna?" I call out, as I watch her leave the desk, failing to respond to anything I've just said.

"Home. I don't feel well" she tells me, leaving the building.

One more week, Christina. Just one more week I need to put up with her bullshit, then she's heading into her day shift job. You can do it, so let it go. Come on, don't let her get to you. It's Friday, you have the weekend off – Don't threaten to quit, just because she's turning crazier on a daily basis.

CHAPTER 6 – *OUT IN THE OPEN*

I've just had the most amazing weekend of my life. Many would think I went out and got myself laid. In-fact, everyone would think this if I said amazing weekend and they knew me. No, no sex whatsoever and almost forty hours on my back, enjoying my bed alone! Yes, I've slept, I've slept some more and I've recharged my batteries fully!

After Jenna walked out on the shift Friday night, I can't say I've given her much thought over the weekend, but I am going to deal with her now It's Monday. I'm sick of her mood swings, sick of her bitchy behavior and now I'm sick that she isn't the boring prude she used to be. Tonight I plan to set her straight. I'm the one turning up in my skirt tonight – I'm the one who is going to be full of confidence – And I'm the one who will say something about those holes, if she's a bitch just once!

On a more positive note, I haven't had any sexual intercourse over the weekend; not even with myself and I don't plan to have either. On Saturday afternoon Mr Brad, sexy ass Noble rang me like he said he would, then set up a date. Now obviously, I wanted it over the weekend, so I could fuck his brains out without Jenna's hole staring at us, but because he's away on business until Tuesday, I've got to keep my legs closed until Wednesday night, when he plans to return to the hotel. Wow, I'm so excited – That's like work tonight now it's Monday, work tomorrow night on Tuesday, then whether the hotel likes it or not, me and him in a room all night long on Wednesday!

Things are really picking up in my life right now, aren't they? A promotion – A week before Jenna leaves the night shift and I have employees under me – Dean joining us on Thursday in Jentina – And as I've already mentioned, the possibility of a new boyfriend called Brad. Have I said or thought about his name Brad enough over the weekend? Brad, Brad, Brad, Brad, Mrs Christina Noble... MM-mm, maybe to soon to be thinking the Mrs Christina Noble part, but Brad, Brad, and certainly Brad again!

7:48pm (Monday 29ᵗʰ March)

"Hello Christina. Have you had a good weekend?" chirps Mr Harper, as I walk into work tonight, thrilled by my mood, appearance and oozing confidence.

"I have, but I've also missed this beautiful place very much" I respond, putting an instant smile on his face, then on mine too, knowing I'm being completely honest when I say it. "No Jenna yet?" I question, quickly realizing she's not behind the desk already.

"No, not yet" he answers. "No, proper uniform on offer tonight?" he throws back at me, noticing my horrible tight trousers have been replaced by my old sexy work skirt again.

Although I know he's not offended or that bothered about me wearing it, I still try to find a quick excuse, but strangely can't.

"It's okay Christina. Wear what you feel comfortable in and... HOLY SHIT!" he gasps in shock, shocking me slightly, him swearing in front of me for the first time.

Yes, that was definitely worthy of a little swear word Mr Harper, because I can't believe my eyes either.

"You guys okay? You look like you've seen a ghost" sings Jenna, walking in to start her shift with me.

Is she wearing a shorter skirt than me? A denim skirt by any chance? Has she got white fishnet tights on? Has her hair magically turned from brunette to blonde over the weekend?

"Look at us Chrisy. People would actually think we're sisters, wouldn't they?" she continues to chirp, obviously not seeing the wrong Mr Harper and I can both see already.

Okay, maybe I shouldn't be speaking for Mr Harper, considering he's getting ready to leave now, but fuck me, what's going on here?

"Girls, I know it's obviously dress down casual Monday or something, but let's try and wear our uniforms to work tomorrow night, shall we?" Mr Harper chirps, heading for the exit.

"Yes Mr Harper, will do" I call out, feeling I was

tempting fate wearing my old skirt, but Jenna's simply gone...

"Yes Mr Harper, will do" she then mimics me, with a huge cheesy smile on her face.

Okay, what's going on? This is a joke, right? First she's wearing a skirt, which although fits her really well, isn't something she'd normally wear. Then what's with the blonde hair, styled just like mine?

"You ready for a great night then Chrisy?" she asks.

Yeah and about that. In-fact...

"Please don't call me Chrisy, Jenna. You know my name is Christina" I politely point out, clearly taking the shit from her, I said I wouldn't be taking from her tonight already.

"Sorry CHRISTINA" she quickly responds, strangely elaborating on my name and calling me touchy instead.

Wow, this is going to be a long night, if I've got to put up with my crazy double driving me insane all night long!

8.42pm (Monday 29th March)

"Good evening sexy ladies. Who wants to get lucky with the Sheen tonight?" Gary Sheen sings out, dancing towards us at the desk with immense confidence.

"Evening Mr Sheen. Room for two?" I respond.

"Evening Mr Sheen. Room for two?" Jenna mimics me again.

Okay, this is now officially creepy. And great, Gary is about to notice it too.

"I didn't know your twin sister worked here, Christina" he chirps, asking if she'd like to spend a few sexy hours alone with him.

On Friday I wasn't too pleased about these two heading

towards a room for sex, but seriously Gary, take her away. In-fact, take her away all night long!

"Chrisy" Jenna whispers beside me.

"Ooh, I like that. Chrisy now, is it?" Gary wades in.

"No, it's not!" I growl, giving Jenna such a dirty look beside me.

"Sorry, CHRISTINA" she then corrects herself, giving Gary some kind of weird looking wink. "How many times have you had sex with Gary here?" she asks me.

"Once and never will I again" I whisper back, having absolutely no idea why this is being asked in front of him, obviously not wanting to offend him with my statement either.

"Now you can ask me, Mr Sheen" she sings out, dancing around sexily in her tiny denim skirt for his benefit.

"Ask you what?" confused Gary responds, shaking his head, whilst beaming from ear to ear about her blatant attempt to flash him some of her knickers.

"Ask me if I want to have some sexual fun with you tonight" she sings out again, swinging her hips and tempting her skirt up even more.

"Would you?" he asks, not exactly putting it into the words she clearly wants to hear, as I quickly start to feel I'm getting in the way for some reason.

"Once and never will I again" she answers, totally copying my answer.

Really? Is that what all that teasing was for? So you could do a horrible impression of me again? What the fuck has happened to you Jenna? You used to be someone I looked up to and kind of respected?

All I can do is stand and watch her check Mr Sheen into

the hotel, as she strangely gives him room eight upstairs, claiming she's going to work backwards tonight and head towards filling room one by the end of the night.

"Whatever floats your boat, freak" I whisper under my breath, already feeling I've had enough of her and we're only just over an hour into our first shift this week.

"Whatever floats YOUR boat, freak" she sings out with a smile on her face, showing me that she heard my little announcement and she isn't bothered by it.

Seriously, this needs to stop. Why is she acting completely normal in front of others, then doing crazy shit around me? Am I the only one seeing it? Am I going insane or something? Can't anyone else tell she's dyed her hair blonde to purposely look like me? That does it... I said I wouldn't put up with her crap and I'm not going to put up with it any...

"Jenna, how's Greg?" I quickly ask, making sure our private little conversation can't be heard by anyone else.

"Wouldn't you like to know?" she answers abruptly, almost snapping out her words at me.

Okay, has she found out about the mistake I made with her man Greg last week? Is this what this strange behavior is all about?

"Seriously Jenna, how is Greg?" I ask again, really wanting an answer, so I can maybe get through to her a little bit.

Okay, a raspberry being blown in my direction isn't exactly the answer I was hoping for. Right, let me put it another way for you.

"Considering you clearly had sex with Mr Sheen last week, I thought that you might have split up with Greg or something" I say, being open and honest about the concern I'm currently sharing, although I wouldn't blame

Greg if he had dumped her sorry ass right now.

"You would like that, wouldn't you?" she responds, almost admitting she knows something, without actually telling me she knows. "How's Greg? He's dead" she adds, giggling to herself about her answer.

Okay, that's not a bizarre thing to say, is it? It's as though it's a joke, yet the seriousness in her face is telling me it's also a lie.

"What do you mean he's dead?" I question playfully giggling, obviously fishing for more information.

Although I don't believe it, I do feel the more she talks, the more she waffles this crap at me, the better chance I've got of getting to the bottom of all this weird shit.

"I mean, I killed him at the weekend for cheating on me" she giggles again, obviously joking too.

I don't know what's freakier – Her saying something terrible like this – Or her laughing at the fact she thinks he's been cheating on her? Or was that for my benefit? Does she actually know about Greg and I, then this is nothing but a wind up to get even with me? Oh good, a couple of guests... You just freakishly deal with these new people entering the building Jenna, and I will nip to the toilet.

9:07pm (Monday 29th March)

Is this really Monday night? Does it seem like my head has been caved in already, as though I didn't just have the weekend off work to rest? Am I really sitting on the toilet right now, not needing to go, yet not wanting to get up either? Is Jenna really going a little crazy, or is it me? Is she doing this on purpose, so maybe I go out of my mind? No, why would she do that? Err, because you sat on top of her partner in a sexual way last week. But that was only for a second, so surely not? Wasn't it? Was it for just a second? Surely she would know, considering she was watching? Unless it wasn't her watching Greg and I and it was in-fact someone like Mr Hodge? Yeah, he seems to know everything that goes on around here, so maybe it was him. Yeah, he said the dangerous ones were always the quiet ones. Was he actually talking about Jenna when he said that? Did he already know she'd gone crazy and...

OKAY, THAT'S ENOUGH, CHRISTINA! - You're sounding like a crazy person thinking all this stuff right now, so stop it. Get your ass off this toilet, get back out there and confront this bizarre situation and the crazy wannabe blonde bitch in the process too. If Jenna continues to fuck with your head or mimic you, come clean about the Greg thing. At least you'll know if you're the one going insane, or whether it's just her dealing with her hurt feelings.

9.13pm (Monday 29th March)

"Jenna, I need to talk to you" I say, entering the reception area, noticing her just finishing off with the latest new guests, as I rudely interrupt.
Good start Christina – Talk about look crazy yourself already now!

As the random couple head off towards room number seven upstairs and I patiently, but frustratingly wait for them to disappear first, I start to lose my nerve completely.

"Did you want to talk to me, Chrisy?" she asks,

128

unfazed by absolutely everything I do or say right now.

Okay Christina – Just say it – Just say anything.

"Have you got a problem with me, Jenna?" I ask, instantly going blank the second words start coming out of my mouth.

"No" she simply answers, whilst staring at me.

Okay, that didn't exactly go the way I was planning it to go.

"Jenna" I mumble, tempting myself to try again. "Do you like to watch people having sex?" I ask, cutting right to the chase finally.

"No" she answers again.

Damn it – This isn't working, is it?

"Jenna" I say for the third time.

"That's enough Chrisy. No more questions, I need a short break" she declares, suddenly standing up behind the desk, telling me to cover for her.

Where the hell is she going now? Why didn't I just have this out with her? Did she really just call me Chrisy again? Am I the one that's going mad?

Unable to believe I'm only just starting a shift with her this week, yet she's managed to get inside my head this much already, I do start to fear for my own sanity watching her walk off. Then I suddenly realize where she's off to, when I notice her take to the new staircase. She's going upstairs to enter the secret passageway, isn't she? She's going to spy on the new couple she's just checked into the hotel, isn't she? Okay Jenna Cole, if you don't want to admit you like to watch, then we're just going to have to do this the hard way.

9.40pm (Monday 29th March)

I have given her almost half an hour to do her watching thing up there, so now it's time to catch her in the act. Although I really want to do this, my ass right now is refusing to move itself from my chair. It's not like I'm worried about how she's going to react, it's more what if she spots me before I spot her. I mean, the last thing I need is to ready myself to open that passageway door, then she comes out again. Okay Christina, it's now or never!

It's definitely now, because I'm on my way up there, aren't I? Yes, I'm definitely now sneaking up the new staircase. Wow, why is my heart beating so loud and fast? Okay, this is it – This is the door – Time to confront her about this issue at last.

As I place my key-card to the lock, then swipe it, I know there's no going back. I try to vision the inside of this little passageway in comparison with the rooms, but I can't do it. All I can vision is the downstairs passageway, where I caught her doing naughty things last week. Do it Christina, do it – Just pull the door open and walk in.

"So this is what you get up to on your break, is it?" I quickly call out, as I find her standing at another hole, denim skirt hitched up, playing with herself again.

"FUCK!" she immediately freaks out, leaping out of her skin, as her concentration on the hole is clearly disturbed by me. "What the fuck are you doing in here?" she asks, pulling her skirt down really fast.

Got something to hide, have you Blondie? Don't stop, carry on, so you can't wriggle your way out of it this time.

"What am I doing in here? What are you doing in here?" I throw the question straight back at her, making out I'm really shocked about what I've found her doing.

"Nothing" she answers.

Yeah, you would say that, wouldn't you? You're hardly going to admit it, are you? WHAT? What are you doing now Jenna? No, don't hitch your skirt back up – Don't place your eye back on that hole – Don't start rubbing yourself again.

"Jenna" I call out, realizing she's obviously shut out the fact I've just walked in here or something.

"Shh, Chrisy" she tuts at me, eye still fixated at the hole. "The couple in this room will hear you if you don't quieten down" she tells me in a whisper.

Okay, not exactly the reaction I was expecting. God damn it Jenna, will you stop playing with yourself, whilst we have a conversation about this!

"What do you think is going to happen to your promotion, if this couple hear you?" she questions me, eye still glued to the hole.

"I'd probably get fired" I whisper back.

"Then there you go – Be quiet" she demands.

Is she really telling me what to do, whilst she plays with herself at that hole? Is she really worried about me losing my job, when I'm not the one who is in-fact watching the guests? Wow, I'm not sure how she's managed to turn this around on me, but... Oh fuck it, I haven't got anything else to say now, have I? Great and now I feel I need to get out of here myself, just because I'm watching her do sexual things, watching them again.

"I'm going for my break Jenna, so watch the desk" I announce, realizing I'm about to lose the battle of yet another conversation with her again.

"Fine, have a good time" she responds, not even looking at me, she's so busy. "Don't do anything I wouldn't do" she adds.

What you do Jenna is wrong, weird and slightly disturbing, yet you always seem to make me feel terrible about it.

10:17pm (Monday 29th March)

I can't believe I'm approaching Dean's bar this early - I can't believe what I've just witnessed – Then more importantly, I can't believe she wasn't bothered I discovered her secret hiding spot. Wow, do I actually talk to someone about this? Maybe I should talk to Dean about it, considering he's going to be working at our hotel very soon. No, what if I scare him off, now I've worked hard to get him the job? Saying that, it's not like he can change his mind now, seeing as this sign on his door is implying the bar closes after tonight.

"Evening Christina, want the usual?" Dean calls out from behind the bar, the minute he notices me walk in.

The place is packed, full of people I've never seen in here before.

"Had sex with any guests tonight?" he playfully chirps, as I reach the bar.

Firstly I tell him that I've met someone I really like and won't be doing the sexual things I used to do anymore. Then secondly, I attempt to tell him about the Jenna thing, but can't.

"Well, well, well, if it isn't Miss Cock-tease" sings a random guy, walking towards me and joining me at the bar.

"Back off Thomas, she's got a man in her life now"

Dean barks at him.

Oh that's right... This is the guy I rejected a few days ago, isn't it?

"Well whoever he is, I'm sure he will be left heartbroken soon, because a girl like this doesn't stay faithful for long" this Thomas guy laughs, trying to upset me.

"That's enough!" Dean barks.

"What Dean, is it you then? Are you the sad-sap believing you have control over the knickers, she can't control or keep on herself?"

Wow, this guy really hates me, doesn't he? Wow, Dean really is my friend, isn't he? Look at him leap over the bar, grab this Thomas guy by the shoulder, then march him towards the door.

"You'll get what's coming to you, Cock-tease. You'll have a big man split you in two purposely very soon" he continues to threaten, as Dean tosses him out onto the pavement like a rag-doll.

Thank god he's gone. Oh, and now every other guy in this place is checking me out. Okay guys, stop staring at me, because I don't know if to blush or cry right now. Wow, maybe I haven't given Dean the chance I should have before, because that was amazing. Maybe he's actually more right for me, than this Brad Noble is? Maybe I'm going to....

"Sorry Dean, what was that?" I find myself asking, like I usually do when I'm not paying attention to someone.

"I asked if you were okay" he says, leaping back over the bar and pouring me a quick drink.

How can I tell him I'm fine about this Thomas guy, I'm happy that I've met Brad, I'm now having naughty thoughts about him standing here questioning me, and

133

that I'm tormented by the whole Jenna thing at the same time?

"I'm fine" I tell him with a smile, knowing my head is far too busy to tell him anything.

$11:15$pm (Monday 29th March)

"Oh well, I'd better get back to work" I tell Dean, after I've had a few drinks with him and helped celebrate his final night in business, hoping he doesn't regret listening to me about the job at the hotel soon.

"See you in a few days Christina" he responds, informing me he's got a lot to do over the next few days, but is looking forward to joining me across the street after that.

As I take my final look around Dean's bar, yet can't see much for all of the drunken people in my way, I decide to leave and head back to the insanity I work with, called Jenna. I'm not going to waste my time with her. I'm just going to do my job and ignore the things she does. Hey, it's not like I've got to put up with her for much longer, is it?

As the air hits me right in the face after the alcohol I've just consumed when I'm outside, I strangely feel something else hit me hard on the dark street too. Oh, nothing else has hit me, has it? But I have been stabbed in the back, I think. Yeah, I've definitely been stabbed. Wow, that wasn't as painful as I thought a knife attack would be and... Hold on, who's behind me with the knife then? Oh no, I hope it's not that Thomas guy? Wow, I hope he isn't planning to rape me and stab me to death. Oh dear, I feel the pain trembling through my body now.

Yes, my legs are definitely feeling weaker.

As I clutch myself where the knife or whatever it was penetrated me, I'm a little concerned as to how wet and bloody my hands are getting.

"DEAN!" I scream out in a pain staking groan, obviously not loud enough to be heard. "Who's there?" I groan out again, trying to turn around to face my attacker.

As I come face to face with the person welding the knife in front of me, another sudden stream of pain rockets through my body, as I'm stabbed again, this time in the stomach.

"Dean..." I attempt to call out again, as I feel my legs buckle beneath me and...

Okay, what's going on now? Why am I now sitting in the dark alleyway beside Dean's bar? Oh, Ouch, that's right, I've been stabbed, haven't I?

"Please Jenna" I groan. "Don't do this" I find enough energy to beg her.

"Do what?" she quickly responds, waving her blood stained knife around in the dark. "I'm Christina, not you, so how can I be doing this to myself?" she asks, crouching down in front of me, messing with my head like she...

Do I keep passing out in pain or something? Wow, who would have thought being stabbed would hurt so much? Okay, what's happening now?

"Is... is... is C... C... Christina okay?"

Mr Hodge, is that you?

Wow, why can't I see properly? Why does it feel like I'm moving now?

"Yeah she's fine Mr Hodge. She's just had a few too many drinks" I hear Jenna tell him, whilst my eyes are forced closed because of the pain.

"Mr... Mr Hodge. Help m..."

CHAPTER 7 – *IN SOMEONE'S VOICE*

I fucking hate you Christina, you disgusting bitch!

"You don't need to do this Jenna. Just let me go and I won't tell anyone" Christina squeals, before asking me where I've taken her.

"You're in your beloved hotel, Chrisy" I tell her. "Down in the basement, nobody has ever been able to open, but me" I add.

As I look into the eyes of this horrible little slut, I feel like stabbing her in the face and finishing her off, but hold off until the good part arrives.

"Why are you doing this Jenna? Why?" she squeals out in pain again, trying to prop herself against the wall behind her.

Oh, and here's that good part now.

"Because you slept with Greg, didn't you Chrisy?" I growl at her. "Because you did the dirty on me, didn't you?" I add, hating her guts the more she makes me say it.

Come on then Chrisy, say the part I know that's going to come out of your disgusting mouth next. Tell me how you stopped once you realized it was him and didn't mean to hurt me.

"Please Jenna, it lasted a few seconds, I... I didn't... I didn't go through with it" she stutters in pain and anguish as I kick her feet away, because I don't believe dogs should be able to stand up.

"AND THAT MAKES IT OKAY, DOES IT?" I growl at the top of my voice, desperately wanting to kill her again now, but enjoying the fact she's bleeding to death in front of me anyway.

"No, no, it doesn't make it okay, but surely if I... If I stopped, it didn't do much harm?" she begs some more.
That's it, I want her dead. How dare she tell me it didn't do no harm.

"Do no harm? DO NO HARM?" I yell. "It broke my fucking heart!" I scream in her face, holding the knife to her neck, as she begs me not to kill her.
As my hand shakes with the knife in front of her throat, it's as though I've got to talk myself out of doing it, so do so by remembering I've got so much more to say to her.

"Do you realize how hard it's been for me to work beside someone like you all this time?" I growl at her, making myself comfy on the floor beside her. "Do you realize how much I've hated watching you throw yourself at different men, whoring yourself out like a cheap tart?" I add.
Oh, nothing to say now Chrisy? Okay then, maybe I should just kill you after all.

"WHAT DO YOU WANT FROM ME? WHAT DO YOU WANT?" she cries out, as I threaten to slit her throat, if she doesn't start talking or explaining herself.

"I WANT YOU TO DIE!" I yell at her.

Suddenly everything turns on its head slightly, because cowardly Chrisy on the floor, finally finds a little courage from somewhere.

"You aren't going to kill me. This isn't you Jenna. You haven't got the guts" she groans in pain, trying to sit up again.

No, it's not me, is it? Okay then, let me show you what is me then.

"Hey Chrisy. Say hello to your little friend, Greg" I announce, removing the sheet I had covering his corpse since the weekend, sitting right next to her blood stained body.

As I watch Chrisy look at him, then him strangely look back at her with his glazed dead eyes, it all comes flooding back to me.

"Aah, isn't this sweet? A little reunion between two lovely cheats" I sing, as she freaks out, screaming the place down, then starts calling for help.

"Seriously Chrisy, you're embarrassing yourself now. I took the left over material from our nightclub Jentina, and sound proofed this basement too" I tell her. "You remember, the nightclub upstairs named after both of us, but you tried taking it all for yourself" I add.

"Have the club, have the club, just please let me go" she starts to cry, finally coming to terms with the fact I do have the guts to kill her, considering Greg is still looking at her from his own afterlife.

"And why would I want to let you go?" I question her, confused as to why she'd ask such a ludicrous thing of me.

"Because I will leave. Leave the hotel. Leave this town.

You'll never have to see me again" she whimpers and begs.

"Yeah but if I kill you right now, I still wouldn't have to see you ever again, would I?" I announce, clearly telling the thick bimbo something she's clearly overlooked with her little plan.

With that she breaks down again, sobbing her little devil worshiping heart out, whilst the blood continues to trickle out of her wounds.

"Tell you what Chrisy. Do you mind me calling you Chrisy now?" I ask, ready to offer her a little deal. "You tell me word for word what you and the dead dick beside you did together, and I will let you go" I add.

"Okay, okay" she panics. "It all started when..."

"Now-now Chrisy. You just remember, I was watching everything, so one single lie and I will seriously cut your throat" I warn her, showing her the knife for a final time.

As blood continues to drip onto the floor, and she once again sits up against the wall in this dirty, horrible smelling dark basement, I ready to listen to her version of events.

"I went into the room to change out of my old uniform, like you told me to do" she starts telling me her story. "Then when I realized there were no mirrors in the room, I walked into the bathroom" she adds.

Okay, you're still alive, keep going.

"As I entered the bathroom, it's there I met Greg" she tells me.

Okay, okay, it's getting interesting now. Tell you what, let me throw some questions in too, just so you don't miss anything out.

"What was my man Greg wearing in that bathroom?" I ask standing up, feeling the need to tower over her.

"He was wearing a towel" she informs me, as though I didn't already know this part.

"Okay, okay, here's the million dollar question Chrisy. Get this correct and you live to fight the rest of the story. Get it wrong and you die" I tell her, as the excitement and adrenaline floods my body. "Did you want him the second you saw his body?" I ask, as I suddenly hitch up my denim skirt, throw my vagina forward, then start rubbing myself frantically in her face, waiting for her to answer the question.

At first she doesn't answer the question; which boils my blood a little, but I think that's due to the fact I'm getting myself off right in front of her and she doesn't understand it.

"WELL?" I shout out. "How did you feel when you saw his body?"

"I wanted him" she calls out, not entirely sure about what I'm waiting to hear.

"More than that, or die" I shout again.

"I wanted to have sex with him right there and then" she calls out, panicking slightly, as she tells her guilty truths.

"MORE THAN THAT" I yell again. "Tell me how it made you feel" I demand, bashing against myself as hard and as fast as I can.

"Horny" she answers.

"MORE THAN THAT!" I yell once more, as the intensity in my body rockets towards the moon.

"Very wet"

"MORE THAN THAT!"

"I wanted to have sex with him straight away" she finally admits, as I orgasm for the first time hearing it, then crash against the wall, fighting off a few aftershock

141

shudders.

Once I've composed myself and caught my breath, I stand up, start circling on my clitoris again, then demand she carries on.

"You're sick" she growls.

Jealous much? Didn't you have an orgasm this time yourself then? Don't you want to live any longer?

"You're mental. You need professional help, Jenna" she continues to growl at me, as though she's in a position to have a say.

"And you need to carry on with your little story, before I end your pitiful little life" I growl back at her, grabbing her face really hard in the process.

Once she's got the message and once I've taken a deep breath myself, it's back to the final part of the story.

"Once I walked into the bathroom, he was standing there in a towel and I wanted..."

"ENOUGH!" I yell. "You've done this part already" I tell her, demanding she skips to the interesting part.

Now please, can we get on with this erotic tale now?

"Once he brushed up against me in the doorway, I really wanted it, but I didn't know he was Greg at the time, I promise I didn't..."

"CHRISY STOP!" I bellow, claiming this is getting harder for me to enjoy, demanding she tells me what his penis looked like.

"It was nice" she answers, looking slightly concerned.

"I MEAN, WAS IT SOFT OR HARD?" I yell, getting angry with her again, as I remove the cloth from the lower half of dead Greg's body to reveal his cheating penis.

She squeals, she freaks out yet again, but I demand she

look at his dead genitals, but she won't do it.

"Was it hard? Or was it all floppy like this?" I yell, grabbing her hand and placing it around his cold shaft, wriggling it around a bit.

"IT WAS HARD, IT WAS HARD" she cries out, struggling to fight me off and let go of his dead penis, as I hold her hand against it.

"Do you know what Chrisy? You're a prude and you aren't going to make me cum again, are you?" I disappointingly groan at her, claiming the end is coming. "But what I'm going to let you do is, leave" I tell her.

"You... you, you are?" she stutters, cries and whimpers all at the same time.

I tell her I'm going to let her walk out of here under two very strict conditions. One, she doesn't ever come back to this town again, which she instantly agrees with. Then two, that she take her half dead body back over to the alleyway and sit there until someone finds her.

"If you go anywhere near the entrance of your friends bar, call out, or do anything else, I will race across the street and finish you off" I warn her, promising I will do it.

"I won't, I won't, I promise" she whimpers again.

"Up you get then" I sing out, pulling her up by her hair and watching as she takes a decade to stagger towards the basement door. "Sit in that alleyway and wait for help to arrive" I tell her again, as she finally reaches the door.
Oh fuck, I forgot something, didn't I?

"Chrisy" I call out, wanting her to wait a second.
Once again, it takes her nearly lifeless body a lifetime to turn to face me again.

"I forgot to introduce you to the other guest staying in my basement hotel" I tell her. "You remember Mr Smith,

143

don't you? Say hello" I add, removing another sheet, to reveal his corpse sitting beside Greg.

"You killed him too, but why?" she asks, falling back against the wall in shock. "He was nothing to do with this" she adds, clutching her chest, as though it's going to stop the bleeding.

"He cheated on his wife with his assistant Lara, didn't he?" I ask her.

She nods her head, but still doesn't understand any of it.

"I hate fucking cheats" I announce.

"B... but... but the police were asking questions about him. How did, how... how?" she starts to stutter.

"Easy" I tell her. "I waited for him to ring his wife for the sixth time that night, then when he came out of his room, stabbed him with this very same knife outside the dining room" I confess with pride.

"The blood" she responds, looking confused. "But the blood on the floor was yours from that cut on your finger" she adds.

"I cut my finger, so you would think the blood outside the dining room was mine" I explain. "And who cleaned his blood up? Who's DNA is all over that cloth I have purposely stored somewhere safe?" I ask, finally hoping I've done enough to make my point, and for her to leave town for good if she survives the night.

With no words left to come out of her big slutty mouth, I feel my job is done.

"Tell on me or get me into trouble, then that cloth putting you at the scene of a crime is found" I blackmail her perfectly, as she finally gets the message.

As I watch her open the door to the basement and leave, I quickly race in front of her, simply to make sure the coast is clear. The hotel reception area is empty and so too is the street outside.

"It was a pleasure knowing you, Chrisy" I sing out, finally watching her leave MY hotel for the last time.

As I stand on the doorstep, watching her stagger towards Dean's bar, I just know she's hoping someone will spot her, but it doesn't happen. For a few seconds, it's as though she's deliberating blowing my cover, so I race over to help her hide away a little faster. I guide her back into the dark alleyway where I first stabbed her, then sit her down on the ground.

"Now comes the final part" I tell her, pulling out my trusty knife again.

"I thought you said you wouldn't..."

"Relax Chrisy, this isn't going to hurt. Unless you move of course" I whisper, forcing her legs open, then placing my knife to her knickers.

With one simple slash to tear them, I then go about ripping open her top, making a few holes here and there and she's finally ready.

"What are you doing? Why are you doing this?" she asks, realizing her slutty uniform is hanging off her body.

"One last thing before I leave you" I announce, pulling a little tub out of my pocket and placing it down on the ground beside her.

"What's that?" she instantly freaks out, as my knife reminds her to stay still.

"Just a little of Greg's goo. Goo, I kept safe before I killed him" I tell her. "We want to make your death look like a rape gone wrong, don't we?"

With that, I smear it all around her knickers, then end it all for her as humanely as I possibly can.

7:52 am (Tuesday 30th March)

"Good morning girls, how are... Oh, where's Christina?" Mr Harper sings out, entering the building this morning.

"I... I... I'm not sure, Mr Harper" I act out the perfect voice for him to believe me.

"What do you mean, you're not sure?" he questions, as I thought he might.

"Well I don't want to be a snitch or anything, but she had a few drinks last night, claimed she wanted to go and meet a man, then went over to her friend's bar" I tell him, making it all sound really convincing.

"Oh well, I'd better have words with her later on then" he grumbles, clearly smiling, but doing his best not to frown about it.

"Mr Harper, would you mind if I went home now? I've been here all night by myself and I'm really very tired" I ask.

I don't actually know what voice I like doing best – The suck up, or the vicious murderer, but I do know I want to go home and have a sleep. Oh well, he's buying it at least.

"Of course Jenna, get yourself off home and thanks for covering for Christina" he responds.

And I hope that's the last time I ever hear her name mentioned again!

Leaving the hotel, I feel very pleased with my nights work. I'm the only person who can get into the basement, Mr Harper values me a little more now, and look... If I stare carefully standing outside this building, I can just about make out the dead girls foot over there, still in the alleyway.

146

"Sweet dreams, Chrisy, Christina"

CHAPTER 8 – *BAD NEWS*

Am I nervous now I've had a sleep today and Christina's body is bound to have been found by now? Not a chance, I didn't kill her, she killed herself. Well, she got attacked, raped and murdered, if I'm going to play out and believe the story I've set up perfectly to roll out over the next few days. Wow, I can't believe even after her death how much I hate her. I can't believe I'm still thinking about the whore, even though she's gone. Still, my life, my work and happiness should all fall back into place when I arrive at work in a few hours time. First things first, I've got to wash this terrible blonde dye out of my hair before I leave for work, and I've got to ready my nice uniform to wear too. Can't have Mr Harper upset with me, considering he might be a little upset by Christina's untimely death.

7:36pm (Tuesday 30ᵗʰ March)

Wow, until I actually arrived at work this evening, I think I might have played down just how this murder might take shape in my head. Look at all the police outside the hotel as I turn up – Look at all the police tape cordoning off the area – And look at the white forensic tent in the alleyway, obviously covering her horrid corpse. MM-mm, I think I might have done something really bad here. Yeah, I think I should have kept her in the basement with the other guys, so none of this would be happening right now. Yet how could I have trusted her down there alone with my Greg?

Okay Jenna, get yourself inside – Remember to look confused about all the goings on and...

"Jenna. Jenna Cole. How well did you know Christina Avery?" some random asshole calls out, which seems to have an immediate knock on effect amongst the crowds of people.

"There she is" I hear another voice call out, as lenses are poked in my face and camera flashes almost blind me. "Jenna. Jenna. Can you tell us when you last saw Christina?"

In an event that I didn't vision plotting this whole situation, I find myself being ushered inside the hotel by a police officer, as though I'm the one in the spotlight or worse still, Christina's murderer myself.

"Oh Jenna, thank god you're okay. Thank god you're here" Mr Harper calls out, scuffling towards me through the packed reception area.

Wow, business has certainly picked up, hasn't it? I've never seen this place so busy. Shame it looks more like a police officer's convention, than it does a hotel lobby.

"What... what's... what's going on, Mr Harper?" I purposely stutter, realizing it's time to become the character I need to play this evening. "Why... why do these people keep asking me about Christina?" I question, making out I don't like the commotion around me at all.

As Mr Harper pulls me to the side, then sits me in the new seating area; that has been moved to the side of reception to allow the traffic of people to move around more freely, I brace myself for what he's going to tell me. MM-mm, I wonder what that's going to be?

"Jenna, I'm afraid I have some bad news" Mr Harper says over the noise, sitting down with me and taking a hold of my hands.

Why, has something happened to one of our guests? Has Mr Hodge died or something?

"I'm afraid Christina was... she was..."

Oh come on you pathetic man, get it out already. Why the hell are you stuttering or shedding a tear for her?

"She was... she was murdered last night" he finally tells me.

Okay, first for the stunned look of silence pose, good - Then for the jaw dropping open routine, check - Now it's time to speak, I guess.

"How... how can... no she can't be. I... I... I was with her last night" I respond, breaking down so perfectly, stuttering Mr Hodge would be proud of me.

After giving me a few minutes to wipe my eyes and stop crying, he finally tells me the police would like to interview me inside Jentina. PERFECT - At the mention of her favorite spot in the hotel and something she was so very passionate about, I find this the best excuse to break down again, as I'm taken through into our little nightclub.

Wow, look at this – This room certainly doesn't look like the nightclub it was yesterday. There are cops all over the place, computers lined up along the bar, and people doing interviews in different corners of the room. If I'm not mistaken, that's her good friend from the bar over there being interviewed too. Wow, I wonder if he's a suspect, I wonder if he actually killed her?

"Miss Cole, take a seat please" says an officer at a table in the corner, where Mr Harper has walked me towards.
Without a single word, looking absolutely petrified, I do as I am told, trying to remember to look as worried as I can possibly look.

"Miss Cole, can you tell me what was said the last time you saw Miss Avery alive?" asks the police officer, getting straight down to business.

"She said she was going for her break over at Dean's bar, and was going to find herself a man" I respond, trying to remember the conversation between us, as though it actually happened.

"And would you say this was a normal thing for her to do?" I'm then asked.
I take a small shameful look at Mr Harper, because I'm horrified to admit I knew what was going on, then spill the beans again.

"She spent an hour every morning over at Dean's bar. Ask him yourself. That's him over there, isn't it?" I question, pointing over towards him.
As I suddenly lose it again and force a few uncontrollable tears from my eyes, the questioning just keeps on

coming.

"You said she went over there looking for a man, Miss Cole. Can you tell me who that man was?" I'm asked next. Here it comes – Here comes the point to which I can show them that she was sexually assaulted and murdered.

"How can I tell you who he was? I didn't know him and don't think Chrisy knew him either" I bark, getting hysterical perfectly at the right time.

Once the interviewing officer has given me a few more minutes to recompose myself, whilst the lovely Mr Harper sits beside me, rubbing my shoulder, I'm ready for the question again.

"If you say she didn't know the man she was meeting, Miss Cole. Can you tell me if this is something she did on a regular basis?" I'm asked next.

And here we are – Rest in peace, Chrisy!

"Yeah, I guess so" I whimper a little, trying to hold back more crocodile tears. "If not over at the bar, then here with guests" I add, blowing her disgusting little habit clean out of the water, knowing my story is going to collaborate with what the barman is telling them too.

"So it wasn't a certain man in particular then?" I'm asked.

"Sometimes yeah, but on nights like this; when she hadn't had sex over the weekend, then it could have been any man she could find" I explain.

"So, she was going to find a man for sex, was she?"

"Her final words to me, as she left the other night were – Any man, any size, I will take anything tonight – I just want him, me, or them all over in that alleyway" I explain, placing the final deserved nail into her coffin, before shuddering, whimpering and guessing that the alleyway is where it happened.

A few seconds later, in a cunning bid not to be in the frame whatsoever, I then take it upon myself to become a little more hysterical.

"Was it you? Did you do this to my friend?" I scream out, faking a lunge attack on the barman across the room, as the police officer dealing with me kindly restrains me.

"It's okay, it's okay, it wasn't anything to do with the barman. He was her friend" I'm told, being handed over to Mr Harper, so he can chaperone me outside for some fresh air.

8:41pm (Tuesday 30th March)

All in all, that was a very successful start to the evening. My performance has seen me clear my name of any involvement in my ex colleagues death and I've currently got Mr Harper outside the building, instructing me to take the night off, because we're hardly going to be open for business.

"Please don't send me home Mr Harper, I don't want to be alone right now" I beg. "Let me stay here at the hotel, so I can find out what happened to Chrisy" I continue to plead, giving him my lost puppy dog eyes so he can't say no.

9:21pm (Tuesday 30th March)

I'm now upstairs out of the way, in room number seven, chilling out. If I open this door and walk out onto the landing up here, I can look over the banister and watch as the chaos downstairs slowly starts to wind itself down. Inside the room, with the door closed, I'm relaxed, happy and content – Outside, with the door open, I'm looking concerned and distressed. Inside, happy – Outside, distressed. Inside, outside, inside, outside.

8:38am (Wednesday 31st March)

I am woken in the morning with a knock at the door. I didn't get undressed last night and don't remember falling asleep, but apparently I did.

"Morning Jenna, how are you feeling?" Mr Harper mumbles, standing there on the landing, looking like hell. I guess you haven't had a sleep like me then?

"Lost... Shocked... Hurting" I tell him, trying to etch a smile to my face for his sorrow fueled benefit.

As he enters my room; or his room considering he owns the hotel, he lets me sit down on the edge of the bed to wake up fully, before filling me in on the goings on down in reception.

"It looks as though she was raped and murdered" he tells me.

"Oh no... no, she can't have... I... no, I should have stopped her from..."

"JENNA, STOP THAT" he grunts loudly. "There's nothing anyone could have done" he adds, telling me I'm not to blame myself.

"But how? How did she get raped if she went out looking for sex anyway?" I question, doing my play-dumb routine rather well too this morning.

"They tell me her clothes were slashed and torn, some semen was found at the scene, and that she was stabbed to death, probably after the attack took place" he

155

explains, as I break down, then he instructs me to go home for a rest.

Does he not realize I've had a wonderful sleep already?

"The police will be gone in the next few hours, so if you don't mind, I need you back here by six this evening" he says. "If you don't want to work, I understand. If you do, then I will call someone in to help you take care of the night shift" he adds.

And now it's time to put my master plan into good use too. Here goes then.

"Mr Harper" I whimper a little more. "Would it be okay if I took the manageress job for the night shift instead? That way I don't have to watch someone else come in and you know... SNIFF, WHIMPER SNIFF, replace my friend" I ask.

Wow, I would accept this request if I was him!

"Sure thing Jenna. Consider it a done deal" he responds.

I mean, how could he have refused?

"And don't worry about getting in extra help tonight. I will be able to cope on my own. I want to cope on my own" I tell him, claiming once again that it would be hard someone else sitting beside me, if it's not my good friend, SNIFF, WHIMPER, Christina.

"If that's what you want" he answers, as I ready to leave and finally go home.

CHAPTER 9 – *LET THE WIFE SLEEP*

I've been up since two this afternoon, partly because I slept last night, then partly because I've been watching this great news story on TV unfold in front of my very eyes. Can you believe in this day and age, someone from my local town has been murdered like this?

"It is said that the nineteen year old woman was dragged into an alleyway beside a bar, before being raped and brutality murdered" - "One man named Thomas Lindsay has been arrested and is being question by police"

I hope they lock you up and throw away the key! Oh well, TV off, time to get myself to work, where today I officially become the new night manageress of the Cure Hotel.

7:52pm (Wednesday 31st March)

Arriving at work today, it seems like nothing has happened. The streets are empty, Dean's bar has a closed down sign on the door and all that remains beside the alleyway are a few flowers and teddy bears where that woman was murdered. Wow, how I hate this. In-fact, let's go and read a few of the messages to find out who they're from and who feels sorry for the whore named Christina.

Rest in peace Christina, you lightened up the darkest hotel
for many years.
Gary x

MM-mm, be careful Mr Sheen or you'll be next. I'm the one that lightens up the Cure, not her!

Forever grateful for all your hard work.
God bless, Mike Harper.

You too Mr Harper? I hope you appreciate me this much, considering I'm still here and alive working for you.

What happened to you was tragic. Yet the biggest tragedy
is, whoever did this to you, is still at large.

MM-mm, not signed by anyone, yet even without the name or stuttering babble, I know this is from Mr Hodge. I can smell his nasty aftershave all over this card.

You will be sadly missed xx

Blah, blah, blah... Yeah, I'm bored with this now. Oops, maybe I should have placed something down myself? Oh well then, here goes – Mr Hodge's beautiful flowers shouldn't go to waste, especially on someone like him. I will just take this piece of paper out of my pocket, then write my own little message to the bitch I hated so much.

Chrisy, I can't believe someone would ever do something so horrible to someone so beautiful. Thanks for all the laughs we shared together.
Love always, Jenna x

How can anyone say I didn't love or care about her now? How could anyone possibly want to frame me for her murder, when I was really her only true friend?

"True friend until she decided to have sex with my wonderful boyfriend Greg" I mumble to myself, spitting on the card, before placing it down on top of Mr Hodges flowers, praying that she will go to hell very soon.

8:08pm (Wednesday 31st March)

"Sorry I'm late Mr Harper, I was just leaving a message across the street for Chrisy" I whimper, heading into reception, where he's sitting behind the desk with his head in his hands.

Mr Harper doesn't respond and looks absolutely drained.

"Why don't you get off home to your wife and let me take care of this place now?" I ask, hoping he will accept, because I'd hate to think what I will do if he doesn't.

"If you're sure you can cope, Jenna" he grumbles, clearly hit by the horrid situation now he's had time to think about it.

Wow, I don't think I've let it hit me yet, considering I'm still waiting for the bitch to walk in looking like a cheap whore late for work again.

"I've got it all covered" I tell him with a smile, claiming it's what Chrisy would have wanted.

Yeah, like I know what that bitch would have wanted!

"Good evening Mr Sheen. How can I help you tonight?" I sing out, as Gary Sheen walks in, whilst convincing Mr Harper to believe in me.

"Oh well, I will see you tomorrow morning then" he grumbles again, heading for the exit. "Any problems or if you find you can't cope, or anyone suspicious comes in, give me a call" he adds, leaving the building.

Thank god for that, I thought he was never going to leave.

"So, Mr Sheen. Are you staying with us tonight?" I chirp, turning my attention back to my first visitor of the night, being the new night manageress asking it.

"No, I just wanted to make sure you were okay, after what I heard today" he responds, offering me his sincere condolences at the loss of my friend.

"I really struggled with it this morning, but life goes on. We've got to keep this hotel running somehow" I tell him, claiming Christina will be sorely missed.

"Yeah, she was a really fine receptionist" he responds. "I couldn't believe it when I heard what had happened" he adds, looking a little down himself.

Oh will people around here take a happy pill or something, because this somber mood is really getting me down now!

"It's okay, you've still got me to flirt with, Mr Sheen" I tell him, trying to let the smile on my face rub off on his.

"What, even if I stay here tonight?" he questions, suddenly perking up a little.

Oops, that was too much of a smile I gave him, wasn't it?

"Even tonight" I confirm, giving him a little wink.

"In that case, I will take that room offered" he chirps at me. "Nothing wrong with celebrating someone's life, than doing it having sex, is there?" he asks, making his grieving intentions very clear.

As I book Mr Sheen in, realizing he's going to take advantage of my vulnerable side; although I haven't exactly got one, there's just one thing I want to know.

"Mr Sheen, are you married?" I ask him, out of the blue.

"Never have been, never plan to be" he responds, pleasing me to the point of promising him a wonderfully sexual night, because I hate cheats and he isn't one.

Good thing really, because I would have hated to kill another person I've slept with so soon after my darling Greg.

8:32pm (Wednesday 31st March)

If checking Mr Sheen into room number one downstairs, then promising him sex tonight wasn't bad enough, I then realize this was a mistake, when I quickly remember this was the room in which I caught Christina and Greg doing the dirty on me, so instantly fear entering this particular room again. Still planning to go through with it however, I let him enter the said room, promising as soon as reception settles down for the night, I will give him a knock.

MM-mm finally, some fresh new faces coming into the building and look, four of them all at once.

"Welcome to the Cure Hotel. How can I help you?" I greet them, as they approach the reception desk.

One man in his late thirties, very attractive - One brunette female of the same age, obviously his wife – And if I'm not mistaken, their two daughters. Yes definitely the kind of guests we now want staying at the hotel.

"Hi, we'd like two rooms please. One for the wife and I and one for the girls" says the man.

"Certainly Sir. And can I take your names please" I respond, ready to type their details into my computer.

"I'm Derek Sullivan and this is my wife, Paula. This is my daughter Casey and her best friend, Marsha"

Oh, the blonde girl called Marsha, isn't their daughter. Oh well, nothing wrong with two friends sharing a room, I guess.

As I give the man and wife room number two, then turn a blind eye to the two seventeen year old girls sharing room three, they're all happily checked in.

"Oh and I'd better tell you" I then say, handing over their key-cards. "Our rooms are half price right now, because our control pads aren't functional yet" I add.

"That's okay, the girls have their phones" he responds, before asking if he can have a spare key-card for his daughter, in-case she wants into her parents room later tonight.

"Certainly, Sir"

8:51pm (Wednesday 31st March)

"Good evening Mr Hodge. Are you staying with us tonight?" I ask, hoping he hasn't checked on his flowers across the street, seeing as I took them for myself earlier.

"I... I... know what you... you did" he stutters at me.

Are you talking about those flowers, or the fact I

murdered Christina? No, how would he know I killed her? MM-mm saying that, he did bump into us that night, didn't he? Wow, I wonder if the police have spoken to him yet?

"Mr Hodge, did you hear about Christina?" I quickly ask him, touching base on the subject, considering unlike Mr Sheen, he hasn't mentioned it yet.

"Yes" he answers, very coldly indeed.

"And have you spoken to the police about it?" I then ask.

"Yes" he answers again, not really telling me anything.

"What did you tell them?" I ask, not feeling intimated by this weird man, but quickly understanding why Christina hated dealing with him so much.

"I... I didn't... tell them about y... y... you being out with h... her" he responds, before asking me at even more stuttering intervals, whether or not his coke request will be attended to tonight.

"Of course it will, Mr Hodge" I respond with a huge smile on my face, knowing he knows something, but I don't know what it is yet.

I check Mr Hodge into room number four; the final vacant room downstairs, just so I can keep a better eye on him tonight.

9:42pm (Wednesday 31st March)

Whilst the hotel is already at half capacity, I'm not expecting anyone else to check in tonight. I'm actually a little surprised that we have anyone staying really, considering what's been on the news all day long. It's now I start to relax, feeling everything is heading in the right direction again. Gary Sheen is expecting my knock on his door shortly, Mr Hodge is just where I need him; right next to the basement door, and the other guests all seem to be taking care of themselves.

"Hi, can you tell me where Christina is please?" I then hear someone ask, whilst my back is turned to the front desk.

I turn, as I ready to answer the question, I'm then a little bit shocked to find the last man Christina ever slept with here at the hotel, standing right in front of me.

"I'm sorry Sir, but who are you?" I ask, obviously not being rude, but not wanting to blab sensitive information out in joyful voice, if it's deemed inappropriate of me to do so.

"I'm Brad Noble" he tells me. "I'm supposed to be staying here tonight, because Christina and I are going to discuss the possibility of becoming a couple" he whispers, as though it's all very hush, hush.

That's what you think!

"Let me check you into room number five upstairs, then I will come and talk to you in a few minutes" I tell him, obviously wanting him to pay up front, before hearing the news or changing his mind.

Hey, I've got to show Mr Harper in the morning that business is on the up now I've become night manageress, haven't I? It's no good me showing him this, without any guests staying.

"She hasn't left the hotel, has she?" he then questions, handing me his payment, worried that he might have lost her somehow.

I bet he won't believe how he's actually lost her, when I tell him shortly!

"As I said Sir, I will come up to your room in a few minutes and explain everything" I tell him again.

Although he looks slightly confused, he heads over to the staircase anyway. I think the way he sees it - Even if she has left her job at the hotel, she should still meet him here tonight anyway. Silly boy!

9:52pm (Wednesday 31ˢᵗ March)

It's not that I hated Christina that much, because I didn't, but I'm going to have to sleep with the man who she wanted to date, aren't I? Call it payback, call it revenge for sleeping with my Greg, but I call it attraction, because he clearly gave me the eye just then, didn't he? Okay, maybe it was him looking at me slightly confused by my suggestion, but nevertheless a nice look either way.

"Are you coming in to join me tonight, or shall I get on the phone and ring a friend?" Gary Sheen calls out, just as I'm about to head upstairs.

"Call one of your friends, Mr Sheen" I tell him, choosing this new guy over seedy Gary, as though there is any comparison.

"But I thought me and you were going to..."

Give it up Mr Sheen, before I tell you that I've had a better offer; not that Mr Noble knows it yet.

As Mr Sheen returns to his room, unfazed by my clear rejection, out pops Mr Hodge to say hello too.

"Do you need something or some help with anything, Mr Hodge?" I ask, taking to the staircase.

"N... no, just t... taking my chair o... out into reception, so I... I can sit d... down" he responds, strangely holding up his room chair to show me.

Although I made it clear to Mr Hodge a few days ago; that no chairs were to allowed to leave our rooms again, I decide to let him do whatever he wants, seeing as I'm not going to let him bother me and I've got too many other things occupying my mind right now.

As I watch him give me strange looks, dragging his limp body and chair over into his favorite corner of reception, I make my way upstairs to Mr Noble's room, ready to deliver him some very bad news; bad news depending on who you are when you hear it.

"Come in" Mr Noble says, opening his door, clearly intrigued by what I refused to tell him at the desk.

As I enter his room and the strong smell of his lovely aftershave hits me, I'm ready to become a better lover than Christina ever was for him.

"So, what was it about Christina, that you wanted to come to my room and tell me?" he asks standing beside his bed, whilst I sit down on the chair beside the mirror and dressing table.

"There's no easy way of telling you this" I tell him. "But Christina is dead" I add.

Wow, that was quite easy to deliver, wasn't it?

As I watch the strong man let his legs buckle underneath him and wobble down onto his bed, I quickly stand up and make my way over to him. I sit down beside him, where it's clear to see he's in shock, so place my hand down on his knee to comfort him.

"How could this have happened? I only spoke to her the other day on the phone" he questions, clearly dumbfounded by the news.

Okay, he's not a man that cries, so that's good. Now, how do I offer him my body?

"She was raped and murdered across the street

166

yesterday" I tell him, as he chokes up a little hearing some more of my devastating news.

"Oh that's terrible" he shudders. "Were you two close friends then?" he strangely asks, heroically worrying about my feelings rather than his own.

I can see why Christina chose to make this guy a permanent thing in her life now. Shame she will never get the chance to have him, isn't it?

"Yeah, we were best friends" I announce, suddenly working out my way into his heart and hopefully his trousers too.

As I break down and start to cry a little, he places his arm around my shoulder.

"The hotel shouldn't be making you work like this" he grumbles angrily, squeezing my arm, then pulling me closer towards him.

"No, no, I wanted to work. It's, it's... it's the only thing keeping me going" I start to stutter and whimper, realizing I have him just where I want him.

Wiping my make-believe tears on his shirt follows next, then the chance to strike.

"If there's anything I can do, just ask" he whispers, taking my face in his hands and wiping my tears whilst looking into my eyes.

I slowly lean towards him some more, then quickly plant my lips against his. Obviously I don't open my mouth, because that would seem a little too forward under the circumstances, but our lips do stay locked together for a while. Then I do it – I do exactly what I need to do to capture him fully.

"I'm sorry, I'm so sorry, I shouldn't have done that" I cry out, racing for the door like I'm ashamed of myself, then leaving before he's had a chance to act.

Okay, I'm on the landing outside his room now. I can hardly go and sit at the reception desk all happy and chirpy again, so let's hide. Quickly, before he comes out of his room looking for me. Stop watching me come downstairs Mr Hodge, you haven't seen me, right? I race towards my favorite hiding place of all, somewhere no-one else can access, then disappear into my secret passageway behind the downstairs rooms. Wow, that was easy, wasn't it? Now all I've got to do is go and apologize later on and the rest should take care of itself. Now, how long shall I hide in here? I guess I could see what our other visitors are doing right now, behind these holes couldn't I?

10:23pm (Wednesday 31st March)

Room one, Mr Gary Sheen. Not much happening in here. Clearly he's sitting on his bed watching TV, waiting for his whore to show up. Maybe a little viewing later on; if I'm in the mood, but nothing that is going to be worthy of my time anyway.

Aah room two, Lindsay the daughter and Marsha the blonde best friend. Wow, for two seventeen year old girls, they've certainly gone to bed early, haven't they? Maybe the family have a big day out planned or something tomorrow? Night-night girls, sleep well.

MM-mm, now we're at room three, aren't we? The married couple. I guess I'm not going to see much of interest in here either, but I might as well have a quick look, considering Mr Hodge's room is next and I don't fancy looking through that hole. Okay, mommy and daddy are in bed; just like the girls are next door and that's about... Ooh wait, what's happening over there? Why is daddy picking up his phone and getting out of bed, whilst mommy is still sleeping? That's right daddy, walk towards me at the wall, so I can see what you're doing on that phone, but mommy can't. Okay, good, he's sat down in the chair and wait a minute, wait for it... There it is - The screen he's clearly come over to hide from his sleeping wife, in-case she... Gosh! Isn't that a picture of a half naked female he's been sent? It's certainly not his wife, that's for sure. Wait a minute, isn't that... Yes, that's the daughters best friend, isn't it? But why would she be sending him a picture like that? Okay, he's sending her a message back now, so let's see what he's got to say for himself.

Marsha, please stop sending me photo's like this... We kissed once months ago, but it's over now.

Okay, at least I know he isn't initiating this sordid situation. Wait, here's a message back from her again. Come on then, move out of my hole space Mr Sullivan, so I can read it with you.

I know you want me. Are you thinking about me in the next room playing with naked body? xxxx

What a dirty little whore this Marsha girl is. That's it, you turn your phone off and go back to bed Mr Sullivan, don't rise to her disgusting and evil temptations. In-fact, let me see if she's actually doing what she says she is, or whether she's lying to you.

As I scurry back towards the hole in the wall next door, I can't believe a seventeen year old would be so sexually direct with her best friends father. Then I see it... The little blonde whore, phone in one hand, whilst playing with herself under our hotel sheets with the other.

"He isn't going to text you back, so there's no point waiting for it, you disgusting tramp" I grunt quietly. "Take your hand out of your knickers and stop doing things like that in a bed, right beside your so-called best friend" I add, feeling my blood boil yet again.

This girl needs to be taught a serious lesson in the value of marriage, because she certainly doesn't... Wait, what's she doing now? Where's she going?

Unable to see much in the dark room and desperately wanting the hole in front of me to grow a lot bigger, I pin my eye to the wall, to find out what she's doing. Yeah, she's definitely getting up – She's definitely doing it slowly, so she doesn't wake her friend. Oh dear, this isn't going to end well, is it? Now she's taking the parents key-card off the side and leaving the room, still dressed in her pink pajamas. Bugger – If I was in reception right now, I would have seen her coming out of the room by now, wouldn't I?

Like a heat seeking missile, I scamper back to the parents hole to find out if the young girl is going to have the nerve to enter the parents room. I mean, what's she going to do, if she does? Hold on... Now daddy is at it beside his wife in the bed. He's clearly holding his phone up, whilst he jerks himself off in the dark.

"I hope your wife wakes up and catches you doing

that" I grumble to myself once again.

I can only guess what you're finding sexual on your phone right now, but I assume I'd be correct if I guessed it was Marsha's latest picture that you were enjoying right now. Wow, I wish someone would turn the lights on in the room, so I can see a little more.

"Oh no, this isn't good" I whisper to myself, noticing the room door open slowly.

Look at this – He's so wrapped up in the picture Marsha sent him, that he hasn't even heard or noticed her just creep into his room. And there go her eyes, almost lightening up the dark room, when she notices what he's doing. Put it away Mr Sullivan, there's a seventeen year old girl in the room with you. Wow, why have I got an urge to bang on this wall and stop this from happening? Saying that, why is the young girl edging towards the bed with every passing second? More importantly, why am I getting nervous about this, seeing I'm not even in the room with them?

Come on, notice her standing there and stop jerking off to her picture. She's literally standing right beside you now and oh, there she goes... She reaches down, puts her hand on top of his jerking hand then... Oh well, at least that has stopped him – At least he didn't jump and wake up his wife, when he was interrupted then. Yes, yes, yes, he's clearly worried about disturbing his sleeping wife now, look... He's clearly trying to take the young girls hand off his erection, demanding she leave. It's at times like this when I wish these holes had audio too, because I can't hear what they're saying from here. Oh dear, she's giving him that look, isn't she? He's not going to be able to resist her in a few seconds, is he? Quickly Jenna, bang

171

on the wall now and stop this crime from taking... Too late!

As I watch an adult male lie in a bed beside his sleeping wife, I can't believe this young hussy has walked into their room and now has her mouth wrapped around his shaft on that same bed. In-fact, cor, this is quite hot really!

I quickly make sure my eye is pinned to the wall in position, then run my hand into my own knickers, getting quite excited about this now. Unable to breath too heavily, I watch as she slurps on his erection, wondering whether the slight rock of the bed will disturb the sleeping wife.

"Go on you little tart, suck him off" I mutter to myself, rubbing hard against my clitoris as I watch. "Bite the cheating asshole's dick right off" I will her to sink her teeth in, but she doesn't.

As the intensity builds in the room and in this secret passage too, I watch as he gets going fully and the bed rocks even more. Wondering whether the young slut is going to climb onto the bed with them, I tease and tempt my first oncoming orgasm to reach it's peak at the same time. Suddenly, I pause and hold my breath – Marsha stops sucking, as the wife is disturbed and rolls over to face them. The look of horror on the husbands face is a picture, as he immediately worries about being caught with a seventeen year old's mouth around his penis.

"That was close" I mumble to myself, knowing that's exactly what he must be thinking too.

As the young whore starts going at it again a few seconds later, knowing one flicker of the eye from the wife facing in their direction will surely get them caught, this strangely makes the situation in the room that little more erotic. I say that, because he's reached out and has placed his hand down the front of her pink pajama bottoms. Look at her suck for her life – Look at him stroking, rubbing or fingering something he shouldn't be touching – Look at this, my first orgasm of the night, rushing through my body, ready to explode. Who is going to cum first? Me, here, watching? The little girl, being fingered by her friends father? Or him, the cheating bastard? Saying that, would the wife climax instantly, if she woke up right now, or would she kill them both?

As we all secretly get into this huge game of cat and mouse, it really is the hottest situation I think I've ever been involved in. As my orgasm continues to grow, I battle against the urge to moan out in pleasure. Inside the room, both of the guilty assholes are struggling to keep their noises to themselves too. Look at her, she's going to explode on his experienced fingers – Look at him, he's enjoying it immensely one minute, then fearing his wife waking the next.

Suddenly, as my orgasm reaches the point of no return, things happen in the room that make me come to a frustrating halt.

"Ooh, I hate being on the verge, then not being able to cum" I shudder to myself, feeling the frustration flow through my body, right down onto my intimate angry nerve. "You've done it now Mr Sullivan" I growl, desperately needing to cum, yet wanting to kill him for it more.

How dare you stop fingering her – How dare you slide

out of bed and point the young slut in the direction of the bathroom. I wanted your wife to wake up and catch you – She's hardly going to do that, if you hide in there, is she? Are you sure you want to do this to my orgasm, Mr Sullivan? You might regret it, you know?

Before I know it, I'm racing out of the secret passageway and towards their room door. If there's no chance in the wife catching them now and there's no chance of me watching what they do next, then what's the point in them carrying on? How dare they think they can do what it is they are doing and not involve me?

As I arrive outside the married couple's room, I immediately tap on the door, then tap louder again. I don't care if I wake the wife up now, there's no way that disgusting man is going to cheat on her like this.

"Hello, what can I do for you?" grumbles the husband, opening the door in an aggressive way, as though I've interrupted his sleep.
Oh, you want to pretend with me, do you? Okay, two can play at that game, Mr Sullivan.

"Please help, there's a fire in the basement, I'm here alone and I'm not strong enough to use the extinguisher" I whisper, letting my Oscar winning panic performance and my sexual frustration do the talking.

"Okay, give me a second" he responds, telling me he's putting some clothes on, yet I know he's going to inform his little hussy inside first.

12:28am (Thursday 1st April)
Knock, knock, knock...

"Where have you been? I've been looking for you everywhere?" asks Mr Brad Noble, as I knock upon his door almost an hour later.

"I'm sorry, I'm so sorry" I almost cry, so he feels the need to invite me inside.

And I'm right, because he does invite me into his room once again.

"Look, that kiss wasn't your fault earlier" he instantly tells me, standing beside his door. "I think the shock of Christina's death got to us both" he continues to explain, clearly trying to explain why it happened for him.

"I... I just can't believe she's... she's gone" I decide to cry at the perfect time, knowing my insides are turning over and my swollen clitoris needs taking care of immediately.

As he wraps his arms around me for the second time tonight, I know this is it. One mistake apologized for, so the next time we kiss, surely can't be a mistake too.

Wow, I was right... One comfort by him – One look of desire from me – And our lips are at it again. MM-mm and now he's throwing me onto the bed – And now my uniform is literally being torn off my body. Wow, I hope my frustrated orgasm doesn't appear as quickly as I fear it's going to, because I want to take my time and enjoy this properly tonight. Are you watching from hell, Christina?

8:05am (Thursday 1st April)

"Shit!"

"Shit, shit, shit!"

"What's wrong?" questions a confused looking Brad,

waking up beside me this morning.

"I'm supposed to be at my desk. This isn't my room, I shouldn't be sleeping" I grumble at him, trying desperately to find my clothes.

As I jump into my trousers, then half button up my blouse, I leave the room, worrying about Mr Harper already being downstairs looking for me.

Okay, what's going on here? Why is Mr Harper behind my desk and there are at least four police officers down there with him? Wow, I hope nothing else bad has happened?

"Mr Harper, Mr Harper, I am truly sorry" I panic, racing downstairs towards him. "I... I... I got upset about Christina last night and must have fallen asleep" I play out perfectly.

"That's completely understandable Jenna, so don't worry yourself about it" he responds, trying to calm me down, with a reassuring hand on the back of my neck, before asking me the million dollar question. "Have you seen Mr Sullivan?" he asks.

It's right here I realize this is the reason for the police stopping in by, because they're clearly interested in my answer too.

"Mrs Sullivan reported her husband missing some six hours ago and hasn't seen him since" Mr Harper continues to explain.

"Oh..." I respond, feeling this is the best time to play dumb again.

As I take in the mini commotion, suss out the four cops standing beside us, then notice Mrs Sullivan and the girls sitting in the seating area too, I know I've got to make my move. I walk over to the desk, lift a few files I deliberately placed there a few hours ago, then show Mr Harper and the police what I wrote down on my note pad.

Mr Sullivan dropped his mobile phone at 11:05pm exiting his room. Make sure he gets it back when he checks out.

Obviously, he didn't drop his phone by mistake, more dropped it when I hit him, but this story will do.

"Do you know where he was going, Miss Cole?" a police officer questions me.

"No, but I did see the young blonde girl sneaking into their room twenty minutes before he left" I whisper, so the family sitting in reception can't hear me.

"Why would the friend of the daughter be sneaking into the parents hotel room?" another office asks, as though I'm supposed to know.

I shrug my shoulders as another one examines the phone, because I set the phone up this way earlier too, the cat is well and truly out of the bag.

"Marsha, can you tell us why you were seen entering Mr and Mrs Sullivan's room late last night?" the first officer turns and asks her.

"I didn't" blonde Marsha responds, looking as guilty as hell, but denying it anyway.

"What a stupid thing to suggest. Why would she enter our room?" grunts the wife, jumping to the young cock-suckers defense immediately.

That's because you were asleep when it happened, weren't you Mrs Stupid?

"The content of this phone suggests she did enter your room and an eye witness has confirmed it too" explains the officer, waving the phone in the air.

"Hey, that's my husbands phone. What are you doing with it?" the wife calls out, miffed for some reason.

Before the police have had a chance to ready her for the distressing pictures and sexual text messages on the husbands phone from Marsha, the teenager starts to blab, like I was hoping she might.

"I'm sorry, we didn't mean it" she instantly whimpers.

"Didn't mean what Marsha? What are you talking about?" the wife questions, as the daughter sits next to her friend in silence.

"It was only a bit of fun, that's all. Nothing really happened, I promise" Marsha continues to spill and share her own beans with everyone.

With that the police quickly intervene, suggesting the whole family accompany them to the station. Seventeen year old slut Marsha becomes number one suspect – The wife suddenly hates her guts – Mr Harper is happy with me again – And no-one is ever going to find Mr Sullivan's body in the basement with Greg and the other cheating guy, Mr Smith.

CHAPTER 10 – *SINISTER KEY-CARD*

With three bodies in the basement rotting away like cut up bits of flesh and Christina's death on my conscious too, that's four murders I've committed and although I can consider myself a serial killer now, I'm actually more proud that nobody has got close to catching me yet. Who's next I wonder? What other cheating asshole will check-in at the hotel tonight? I'm going to have to think up a better plan soon, otherwise those bodies I'm leaving around are going to stink the place out.

On a more refreshing note, I'm over the moon about my night with Brad Noble. Although I had to bail out on him pretty fast this morning; just in-case I needed an alibi for the night, he's certainly something I will never regret, not that I regret killing any of the asshole's I've killed already. Although thinking that, I feel I should have killed that Marsha girl too, because in a way she horribly reminded me of Christina the slut, who would also do anything for a man's attention. Wow, how Christina's funeral next Tuesday is going to be fun. I might have to buy myself some eye-drops to make myself cry and look upset. MM-mm, I wonder which one of her friends or relatives is going to comfort me on that day?

Oh well, Thursday is here and I'm just arriving at work. With a murder across the street and a man going missing last night, this place has certainly started to turn into a ghost town all of a sudden. Well, except for this guy coming towards me now. Wow, isn't that... Isn't that Christina's old friend from the bar across the street?

"Hi, you must be Jenna" he says, meeting up with me outside the hotel entrance. "I've heard a lot about you" he adds, before lowering his head, realizing Christina must have told him all this stuff and she's dead.
I bet none of it about me was nice, was it?

"So what are you doing here? Are you planning on staying at the hotel tonight?" I ask, because it's clear he's coming inside with me.

"No, I work here now" he beams in response.
Oh no you don't!

"Hi Jenna, Hi Dean" chirps Mr Harper from behind my desk, welcoming us both in for some strange reason.

"No-one told me this guy was going to be starting here tonight" I calmly say, hiding the disappointment I feel about this decision being made.
Once Mr Harper has assured me I must know, then doesn't believe me when I tell him I don't know anything about it, it all becomes a lot clearer.

"That's right" he tries to laugh. "This was Christina's night shift and Dean working here of an evening only meant she needed to know" he adds.

So, I have no choice than?

"Don't worry Jenna. I will only be working in Jentina. You won't even know I'm here" says downbeat Dean, fearing I'm not best pleased about his appointment.

And he would be right to think this!

"No that's fine, I just didn't know" I respond, trying my hardest to pin a smile to my face.

A smile I only just manage, before Mr Harper wipes it clean off again.

"Dean's going to need access to the basement at some point later on tonight, so could you try unlocking that door for me again?" he asks. "He just needs to set up the bar taps that need to be placed down there" he adds.

"Sure, I will give it a go" I announce, hiding my worry straight away.

"If not, then I will have to call someone in to replace the whole door" he adds.

Okay, that gives me a few days to sort out my immediate storage problem.

"Or I could just kick it in tonight, if you want?" Dean chirps up, acting all macho and suck-up.

I could just kick it in tonight, if you want – What a dick! Who does he think he is, coming in, already feeling he can take over?

"Let Jenna try the door again tonight and if she doesn't get anywhere, I might take you up on that offer" responds Mr Harper, obviously loving this guys enthusiasm more than me.

As Mr Harper gets ready to leave and go home to his wife for the night, I quickly catch him at the door, because I need to ask him something in private. I make sure Dean has disappeared into Jentina first, then fire my question at him.

"Have you heard any more news about the Mr Sullivan disappearance yet?" I ask.

"Strangely enough Jenna, I have" he responds. "Although the young girl admitted to having an affair with the married guy, no-one has seen him since" he adds.

"Oh..." I respond, putting on my concerned face.

"Don't worry about it Jenna, it's got nothing to do with the hotel. Chances are, I don't think his wife wants him found now anyway" he adds, telling me all I need to know.

$9:12$pm (Thursday 1ˢᵗ April)

Wow, I can't believe no-one has come in tonight yet. This is going to be a really slow night, if someone doesn't take a room soon. Saying that, it's going to be even slower for Disco Dean, considering he's been hired to run a nightclub, without a single night clubbing person in sight. Oh and here he comes... That's it Mr Barman, do your strut in my direction.

"Would you like a drink, considering no-one is in yet?" he asks with a friendly smile, exiting Jentina.

"Do you think it's wise us drinking on duty?" I snap at him, playing out my manageress role to perfection.
That shut him up, didn't it? Off you pop then Disco Dean, back into your cave for the entire night now!

"When do you think you will be able to try that basement door for me?" he calls out whilst walking away from me.
Damn, I forgot about that, didn't I?

"Tell you what. Let's have that drink, then sort out a time out, shall we?" I call back, needing his mind off the basement door permanently now.

The way I see it... He can either leave my basement door alone, or kick it in. Alone means he stays alive – Kicking it in means he will force me to help him join the gang already down there. Oh good, finally some guests.

"Hello, welcome to the Cure Hotel. How can I help you?" I ask, as a couple approach me at the desk.

"Double room for the night please" says the man.

Okay, what have we here? Is he going to be my next victim? Only a cheat dies remember, Jenna!

"Can I ask for your names, please?" I question them, knowing I need to punch their details into my computer, which will then confirm if they're married or not.

"Harry Bentley and Diane Cortes" he announces.

Oh dear, I hope you guys are engaged to be married then. I would hate to think you've come here to cheat on your partners.

"Okay, that's you booked in" I tell them, handing over the key-card to room number one. "And can I ask, what brings you guys into town?" I quickly ask, claiming I'm doing a little research for the marketing department, knowing full well we haven't got one here at the hotel.

"Just visiting the area" this Harry guy responds.

Damn, that told me nothing, did it?

"Oh, so you're not in town to get married? Not in town for a friends hen party or anything like that?" I ask, pointing over to Jentina, claiming we have a great night spot here in the hotel.

"No, we're not married" laughs the guy, quickly finding my line of questioning a little strange. "We used to be married, but we're not now" he adds.

Okay, so we've got a divorced couple, trying to patch things up. That's nice. That's not worthy of a killing tonight.

"You guys have a pleasant stay" I beam with pride, loving the fact some people can really make me happy.

As I watch the couple turn towards their room, Dean emerges from Jentina with two drinks in his hand, it's then my nightmare comes crashing down around my ears.

"Okay, you go and ring your husband and tell him you're staying over at Tina's house tonight, and I will warm up the bed" I hear this guy called Harry say to the female called Diane.

Dirty lying bastard. Ooh, how you nearly had me fooled for a second there, Dirty Harry. It's one thing getting back together after you've divorced, but it's another to steal another man's wife away.

As quickly as anything I let the rage inside my body flood my brain, then wave Dean off, claiming I will meet him in Jentina in ten minutes time. Once he's turned his back - Once I've watched the female called Diane exit the hotel to use her phone - I make my cunning move.

"Excuse me Mr Bentley, but could you give me a hand lifting a table from our basement?" I call out. "I'm here alone tonight and don't think I can manage by myself" I add.

Although I can tell he's not really interested in helping me, the ego and man in him just can't refuse a damsel in distress, so he starts to follow me.

That's it puppy, keep coming. Just let me open the basement door and I will...

"Bye, bye Mr Bentley, enjoy your trip" I whisper in my

evil killer voice, pushing him down the stairs. "Not dead yet?" I call out, closing the door behind me, following him down the stairs into the basement.

As his injured body lies on the stone ground and he groans in pain, I'm not sure what I'm going to do with him yet. After all, usually I watch them cheat through the bedroom hole before ending their lives, so this is a first for me. Knowing he's dazed, confused and has at least one broken leg, I drag him over to the other dead guys, then sit him up next to the sheet, which is covering the already deceased.

"What happened? Did I... did I trip or something?" he grumbles, trying to find his bearings.

"Yes Mr Bentley, you had a nasty trip, but you're going to be okay now" I sing out, patronizing him a little. "That's of course unless you lie to me right now" I quietly growl, pulling out my killers knife and placing it against his throat.

"What are you doing? What is this?" he instantly panics, feeling his broken leg for the first time, as I place my knee on top of it, applying instant pressure.

"Here's what this is Mr Bentley" I whisper, placing my face close to his. "You're going to tell me what you're doing here with Diane tonight, or I'm going to kill you" I threaten, in my calmest voice possible.

"You think I'm scared of you? A woman?" he laughs with the knife pressed against his throat, as though he thinks it's a toy or something.

Oh a sexist cheat too – Extra pain for your death then!

"You should be" I then growl at him, pulling the sheet to reveal the three dead guy's faces, to enable him to freak out like he should be by now.

I said freak out a little bit, not wet yourself and cry like a baby, Mr Bentley.

"Now I've got your full attention, tell me what you're doing here with Diane tonight, or join the other cheaters" I threaten once again, pointing my knife in the dead's direction.

Wow, isn't my Greg looking a lot more dark and handsome now he's been cold for a few days? MM-mm, that gives me a kinky idea... Okay, maybe an idea for later, once I've finished with this squealing asshole first.

"I... I.... I don't know who these guys were, but I'm not a cheat like them" he immediately cries out, begging me to let him go.

"LIAR!" I yell, jabbing my trusty knife right through his chest, before telling him he has one final chance to tell the truth.

"I am telling the truth, I'm not lying. I'd never cheat on my wife" he screams in pain, gasping for breath, as the blood starts to ooze out of his body.

Just as well I sound proofed the basement, because this guy is definitely a noisy one, isn't he? Oh what was that, you're married too? That makes it even worse, considering I thought Diane was the married one.

As I stab him in the thigh because of his latest attempt to deem me stupid, I warn him the next stab will be fatal. He takes his time, or catches his breath; considering he's in so much pain now, then delivers what are possibly the last words he will ever say to another human-being.

"I love my wife, I wouldn't cheat on her. I don't know what you're talking about?" he yells.

"Silly Mr Bentley – Bad Mr Bentley – Dead Mr Bentley" I sing out, lifting the knife high in the air, then plunging it

186

down with force through his neck.

As he screams in pain one final time, his body instantly crashes to the ground waiting to die.

"You should have told me the truth. Maybe then I wouldn't want to kill your little hussy friend Diane too" I yell in his face.

Hold on... He's gargling something. What's he trying to say now?

"Diane... Is my... is my wife" he mutters, coughing up blood in the process.

"No she isn't, she's your ex wife and you're cheating on your current wife" I yell at him, crouching right down to hear his final words.

"We were... Playing... Playing out a fantasy" he says, shocking me to the core, before taking his last breath and dying.

"Okay, you're not dead, it's okay, you're not dead" I panic to myself a little bit, shaking his arms around in the air.

This was just an honest mistake, that's all. Oh please forgive me Mr Bentley – How was I supposed to know you two are kinky this way?

Hoping the bleeding to death guy lying in front of me has just passed out and hasn't died yet, I desperately try to wake him up, fearing I've made a huge mistake and killed an innocent man.

"Come on Mr Bentley, open your eyes" I beg, strangely opening them for him. "There you go, you can see again" I sing out, asking dead Greg beside him what he thinks I should do next. "Good idea Greg, I will do that then" I continue to babble, hoping the plan I've just heard Greg telepathically tell me is going to work.

I reach down for Mr Bentley's belt and start undoing his trousers. I then pull his pants down over his bulge and take out his floppy penis. Then I stand up, quickly remove my trousers too, then proceed to lower my body down onto his.

"This better work Greg, otherwise I'm going to kill you" I growl, holding the unconscious or dead man's penis in my hand, then guiding it in between my legs. "Come on Mr Bentley, come on. You're kinky like this, so fuck me whilst my boyfriend Greg is watching" I insist.

Although I know I'm not feeling much growth downstairs, or much of a response from this guy, his penis is big enough to stay inside me all by itself, so I begin to ride it. Soon enough, I begin to get off too, as Greg's eyes watching me fuck another guy turns me on slightly.

"Fuck me Mr Bentley, fuck me hard. Make my Greg cum in his pants, as you give it to his future wife hard" I call out, as my oncoming orgasm builds. "Stop fucking bleeding and start cumin, you asshole" I add, getting a little bit angry by his reluctance, as I ride him as hard as I can, then ask Greg if he likes what I'm doing in front of him.

Suddenly it's all over, as I feel my insides tighten, then explode all over his motionless body.

"You did this Greg, you did this. It was your idea" I cry falling from Mr Bentley's body, realizing he is actually dead. "You and Christina are to blame for this, not me. I didn't ask to be cheated on" I continue to cry out, getting slightly hysterical if I'm honest.

Okay, maybe the word slightly is in-fact slightly an understatement, realizing in my mini tantrum towards Greg, I've just taken my knife to Mr Bentley's genitals and hacked them off, but who can really blame me? Oh dear, what have I done? Why am I sitting here with a dead man's penis in my hand?

"Yeah, that's right? So I can slap my horrible boyfriend Greg around the face with it" I snap again, watching as all the blood and gore from Mr Bentley's penis soak Greg's face. "You did this you asshole. You turned me into this" I cry out once again, forcing Greg's mouth open, then shoving the remaining parts of Mr Bentley down his throat, asking him what it feels like to give oral sex to a man.

"You gay freak" I huff at him, finishing off. "You're dumped" I add, claiming I can't date a bi-sexual corpse any longer.

9:52pm (Thursday 1st April)

Thank god there's a running water tap in the basement, because I don't think I would have got away with that, covered in so much blood. The water down there also makes for good cleaning of the floor, so the place doesn't end up looking like the back of a butcher's shop.

Okay Jenna, you've cleaned yourself up, so it's time to open this door, sneak back into reception, then carry on with your night. Damn you, kinky couple's... You should all be murdered for confusing me like this!

Okay, the door is open, but there's a slight problem.

"Wow, you managed to open the basement door then, did you?" calls Dean, seeing me exit the basement and then me strangely tell him no.

"Get that drink ready for me and we'll have a look at the basement in a little while" I call over, claiming I've got to do something behind the desk first.

Oh and there's Miss Cortes, or is it Mrs Cortes, or Mrs Harry Bentley, if I'm going to believe what Harry Bentley told me before he died?

"Excuse me" she calls, standing outside her room. "You haven't seen my husband, have you? He's left me here without the swipe key thing" she asks, confirming my worst fear.

"No Mrs Kinky. I mean, Mrs Bentley – Cortes, I haven't seen him" I respond, not knowing what to call the stupid fantasy seeking woman, as I get my knickers in a twist.

"Would you mind opening my room door then, so I can wait for him inside?" she asks.

Fancy wanting to pretend you're not married, but you are, then checking into a hotel with a stranger, who is really your husband. Fucking people!

"Certainly" I respond heading over and swiping the door open for her. "I'm sure he's only popped out to the shops or something. I bet he won't be much longer" I suggest, crazily hoping I'm right.

With the coast finally clear, it's now time to work on my alibi for the night, so I head across reception to Jentina and decide to have that drink with Dean at last. Now obviously, I don't drink like Christina used to and when I say I don't drink, I don't drink alcohol full stop, but tonight it must be done – Tonight, I've got to down the

Vodka waiting for me on the bar, but before I do, let me just say one thing to smiling Dean.

"I shouldn't really be drinking" I tell him, with an instant smile plastered firmly on my face.

"One isn't going to hurt, surely?" he responds, handing me my glass.

"Yeah, but once I've had one" I say, tipping the horrible tasting liquid down my throat. "I just can't stop" I add, quickly picking up the bottle, then pouring myself another one.

Now obviously I don't intend to drink this next glass; otherwise I might find myself out of it, but I do have a little plan up my sleeve.

"How about you go and lock the front door and I will turn the music up?" I suggest, claiming we aren't going to have anymore guests in tonight, so we could have some fun, before he needs to go down into the basement.

Now obviously again, this is a long-shot, but knowing it's Disco Dean's first night working here, he's hardly going to argue with me, is he? And with that, he's off towards the main entrance to close up for the night. Then whilst he's out there, it's time to empty this horrible Vodka bottle into another bottle and fill it with water. This will be my beverage for the evening, whilst Dean is going to be drinking whiskey and plenty of it.

The second the main door is locked, I crank up the music and hand him the drink I've poured for him. Instantly he takes a sip and almost chokes, instantly I show him I'm a better drinker than him, by downing my Vodka come water in one, so he feels the need to keep up. Now for the second half of my plan.

"Dean, pour me another LARGE Vodka, I just need to

close down the computer in reception" I tell him.

With that and watching him relax holding his whiskey fueled glass, I exit Jentina and race across to Mr and Mrs whatever their names were again, room.

"Oh hi, have you found my husband for me?" Diane says, answering the door to me.

"Kind of" I answer, asking if I can come inside for a minute, knowing they like kinky games, so this should be easy to set up.

10:36pm (Thursday 1st April)

That's stupid Diane taken care of for just now, so it's back over to Jentina to get Disco Dean hammered, then hopefully make him forget about the basement.

Another drink follows another, then another, as I start to act being drunk, then Dean does his best to remain sober and manly in front of me.

"Dean, are you single?" I purposely slur, as we sit down at the table with our bottles.

"I sure am" he answers, slurring a lot more than me, whilst his head starts to sway around.

"But I thought you and Christina had a thing going once?" I question him again, knowing exactly where I'm heading with this comment.

"We did once or twice" he answers, letting the mention of her name get him down slightly.

Okay, here's where this plan falls into place perfectly.

"She was really bad, wasn't she? I mean, really naughty" I giggle, claiming our sex conversations never ran dry of an evening thanks to her.

"She was incredible" he answers, smiling about this

part too. "Why, what did she used to tell you?" he questions, just as I thought he might.

Men are all the same – They just can't resist letting their egos do the talking for them!

"She told me that you were an amazing lover" I tell him, obviously lying through my back teeth, whilst pouring him another drink. "In-fact, she told me so many hot stories about you, that I actually fancied you myself, without even meeting you" I tell him.

Here it comes, the ego in all its full glory.

"And now you've met me, do you still fancy me?" he slurs, trying desperately to focus on my face.

"I sure do" I answer, with a huge flirtatious grin.

"MM-mm, then maybe... maybe we should do... do something about that" he flirts, clearly unable to string two words together now.

"Maybe we should" I respond seductively, standing up at the table, telling him to make a move on me with my eyes.

Okay, the table moving and his chair falling backwards wasn't part of my plan, but here he comes. Now to finally have this night go my way at last.

"You ready for me, big boy?" I whisper, cupping his bulge, as he stands in front of me.

"I sure am" he responds, putting his arms around me, ready to go for it.

"Oh damn" I call out over the loud music still playing. "I'm on my period" I announce, as he falls back into another chair, obviously dejected by my fake admission.

Once I've apologized over and over again, I then declare I want to make it up to him.

"There's a kinky couple I know staying in this hotel tonight. The wife is currently alone right now in her room, waiting for a stranger to go and have sex with her" I explain.

His first raspberry blowing and drunken giggle weren't part of the plan either, but I quickly tell him how much it would turn me on, if he let me watch, then he's as good as in the room with her already.

Minutes later I find myself walking back over to Diane's room, hoping it just falls into place. I told her earlier that I'd seen her husband and he really wants her to try this stranger thing out. Although she was reluctant at first, I told her he thought she might be, so sent over a bottle of Vodka for her to drink really fast; which was obviously the Vodka I refused to drink at Jentina. If she's taken the bait, if she's done what her husband has asked her to do, whilst he apparently waits in reception for her to accept, then this is going to be the alibi I need for myself tonight.

I swipe the key-card at her door and just as requested, the lights are all turned off.

"Is that you, Mr Stranger?" she slurs from the bed.

Good, she drank the Vodka, I think to myself, before giving Dean a nudge in the ribs to speak.

"Yeah, it's me" he answers, as I guide him towards the bed in the pitch black, telling him in a whisper that I'm already horny.

With that he climbs up onto the bed like the trained dog he now is and she's ready for him too.

"Dean, I'm watching. I want you to fuck her" I call out, making my way back towards the door. "Diane, your husband is sitting here with me right now, watching everything you're doing" I then tell her.

"Is he?" she calls out, as I hear them wriggle around on the bed together and zips being undone.

"He just asked me to ask you, if he can finger me, whilst he watches you fuck another man" I call out, confirming his pretend presence.

"Finger her Harry, finger her... MM-mm, oh yeah..."
And there they go... Having sex just as I planned it!

7:41 am (Friday 2nd April)

Unlocking the main entrance door again was the easiest part of my night, but that only came after I watched the couple have sex in the dark at my secret hole in the passageway, then them pass out together.

"Morning Jenna, how was your night?" calls Mr Harper, entering the building first thing.

"Eventful" I tell him.

"Oh, how so?" he questions me, instantly looking puzzled at my response.

"That new guy you hired for the bar, made a pass at me" I tell him. "Then when I turned him down, he got drunk and entered one of these rooms with a female guest" I add, giving my honest version of events, which aren't that inaccurate if you think about it.

"Are you sure about this, Jenna?" Mr Harper questions me again, heading straight for the room I'm pointing at.

"Absolutely" I respond following behind, wondering what he's going to do about it.

"So I'm not going to open this door and find an innocent couple sleeping in here together then?" he asks, ready to open the door.

"Dean is definitely in there with a woman" I tell him.

Obviously this is all he needed, because with that he swings the door open and there they are.

"Mr Harper? Jenna? What happened?" Dean grumbles, trying to open his eyes next to this female called Diane.

"You're fired, that's what's happening" yells Mr Harper, absolutely furious at him.

"But it's not... Jenna, tell him what happened" Dean starts to beg, still trying to work out what's going on himself.

"Don't involve her" grunts Mr Harper. "Did you or did you not try it on with Jenna last night?" he asks.

"Yeah err, I did, but she was on her period" Dean answers, being as honest about it as he can, but not realizing the hole he's digging for himself right now.

"What and then when she turned you down, you thought you'd jump into bed with someone else?" Mr Harper continues to bark at him, as I stand gobsmacked by the whole thing.

"What's going on? Who are you people? Where's my husband?" Diane squeals, waking up beside a man she's never seen in the daylight before.

"And furthermore a married woman, Dean?" Mr Harper growls. "I want you out of my hotel in the next five minutes, or I'm calling the police" he bellows.

CHAPTER 11 – *CAMERON HOLLYWOOD*

To be perfectly honest, as I wake up on this bright and beautiful Friday afternoon, I don't know what I'm more pleased about – Killing all these cheating men, or setting Disco Dean up and having him fired. The one thing I am however slightly ashamed of is killing the guy called Harry Bentley. At first I blamed the couple for getting into what I can only describe as a weird kind of fetish thing, but now sleeping on it, what's wrong with a little fantasy to spice up your sex life? No, I shouldn't have killed this guy or set his wife Diane up like that, but beggars can't be choosers, so I need to learn to live with my...

"HOLY SHIT, what was that?" I call out in an instant panic, hearing a huge thud at my front door. "OH SHIT, there it goes again" I add, racing through into my hallway, not knowing what to do.

"OPEN UP MISS COLE, IT'S THE POLICE" I hear a voice call from the other side of the door, as another loud thud against it follows and I fear it's going to be kicked in at any second.

Okay Jenna, okay, you haven't done anything wrong and you've got the perfect alibi for everything that's happened so far. That's it, walk towards the door and open it.

"Excuse me, what can I do for you?" I growl, as another police officer threatens to put his boot through my now open doorway.

"Miss Cole, we have reason to believe you are connected to the murder of Christina Avery and could also be linked to the disappearance of a few other people" another police officer calls out, telling me that my apartment is going to be searched, as teams of officers push past me.

"This is ludicrous" I yell, demanding them all out of my apartment right now, as though they are going to listen.

As an officer holds me against the wall and reads me my rights, I really can't understand how it came to this. I mean, I had everything covered, so what did I miss?

"I'm telling you officer, you're making a big mistake here" I insist, claiming I need to get ready for work, because Mr Harper is expecting me.

"A big mistake considering we have an eye witness to the murder?" he responds, shaking his head as though he doesn't believe me.

As quickly as I can say the word "Who" faces pop into my head, as I try to work it out for myself.

"I... I... I told... them" Mr Hodge suddenly says,

standing outside my apartment with two other officers.

"You're going to believe this deluded old man, over me, are you?" I bark at the officer still holding me, claiming this is insane.

"Y... you like to... to watch J... Jen... Jenna. I like to... to watch and take p... p... pictures" Mr Hodge stutters once again.

Just like before, I wrack my brain for answers to his comment, then try to work out what he could have possibly witnessed or taken a picture of.

Suddenly, I panic...

"DOWN EVERYONE, she's got a gun" calls the officer who was holding me, as I lean over and take his gun from his holster.

With that I point the gun towards the front door, watch everyone except old Mr Hodge dive for cover, then start shooting. Mr Hodge takes the first bullet, then my second or third shot hits one of the officers outside, as I decide to make my getaway.

As I run down the hallway of my building, knowing the exit out into the street is right in front of me, I choose to take to the stairwell, realizing there's going to be a police presence waiting for me outside too. I head towards the roof as quickly as possible, whist voices and footsteps give chase, then as I come to the roof top door, I start firing at another person standing in front of me.

"Greg?" I question, watching his already dead body take one of my bullets, then fall to the ground and die yet again.

"Give yourself up Jenna, before you turn into a..."

"WHAT THE FUCK?..."

What kind of dream was that supposed to be? Look at me, soaking with sweat, waking up in my apartment after the worst nightmare I've ever had.

"At least you... you c... can have n... nightmares" says Mr Hodge sitting at the foot of my bed, claiming Christina can't have this luxury now she's gone.

Okay, is this real or another nightmare? How can I wake up from a nightmare, if I'm still in that nightmare?

"Mr Hodge?" I question, unable to work it out.

"YES!" he growls at the top of his voice, waking me up fully.

Okay Jenna, get your head sorted. You're awake now, so no more freaking out. These are the clothes you were wearing to bed last night, this is your apartment, so this is the real deal right now. How can... Suddenly I find myself collapsing to the floor and bursting into tears.

"Why? Why?" I call out. "Why did you have to cheat on me, Greg?" I scream, instantly hating my life.

It turns out killing Harry Bentley has really got to me. He was the first innocent man I've ever killed – He should be the guy haunting my dreams for the rest of my life, not Mr Hodge – And to be perfectly honest, there's no way to correct this mistake I've made. In-fact, he shouldn't actually be down in that basement at work with all the other cheats, so tonight I'm going to get him out of there and give him the send off he really deserves. Fancy checking into a hotel with your wife, pretending you're going to cheat on each-other. I mean, who does that? I would, that's who – If Greg was still alive and we could do it of course. Oh Greg, why did you have to cheat on me? Why couldn't we do this pretending to be strangers thing, instead of you sleeping with Christina the way you did? Tell you what Greg, once I've given Harry Bentley a dignified send off tonight, I will make it up to you. Let's try this pretending fantasy thing – Let me see if I can turn you on with it.

7:57pm (Friday 2nd April)

"Evening Jenna. How are you feeling today?" Mr Harper asks, welcoming me into work like he always does.

"I'm fine thanks, Mr Harper" I respond, unable to work out why he's looking at me so differently this evening.

Oh no, perhaps he knows something – Perhaps he's unlocked the basement door himself today and found all the bodies – Perhaps I'm still dreaming and this is going to turn into another one of those nightmares.

"Jenna, the weekend is upon us, so why don't you take tonight off and start your two day break early?" he suggests.

Okay, there's definitely something wrong here. Why do I have the feeling he's trying to get rid of me?

"Seriously Mr Harper, I'm fine. I want to work tonight" I tell him again, putting the widest smile on my face, to prove I don't need to start my weekend early.

"Okay then Jenna, if you're sure" he responds, doing the same smile at me, yet the face he's pulling looks quite terrifyingly worried.

No, I don't like this one bit. Even if he leaves right now, I'm going to be wondering all night long, aren't I? I've got to ask – I've got to ask what's on his mind, haven't I?

"What's wrong Mr Harper? Why do you think I should take tonight off?" I question him, bracing myself for the answer.

"I just thought you might appreciate the break" he answers. "Christina, the police presence, running this place alone, then Dean trying it on last night" he continues to explain, listing everything that might have drained me more than it should have done.

Thank god for that – Mr Harper is just worried about me after all.

"I got up today, I put my uniform on and I'm here on time for work" I point out, showing him I'm of sane mind and one more night isn't going to break me, before my weekend off.

"Yeah about that" he strangely responds, pulling that same funny face. "What do you think you're wearing this evening, Jenna?" he asks.

"I'm wearing my uniform?" I answer, questioning his question myself, unable to work out why he would ask such a bizarre thing.

"Yes you are wearing it, Jenna. That's if our uniform was a schoolgirl outfit" he says.

Oh my... I did, didn't I? I'm wearing a schoolgirl uniform, aren't I? Quickly Jenna, think of something clever to say, otherwise he will have you sectioned, not just sent home to rest. Why would I turn up for work and not notice what I've put on?

"Oh yeah..." I giggle, looking down at it.

No, I've got nothing to offer him, have I? Unless I want to confess I dressed up like this for Greg's sake, because I'm planning to do this pretend fantasy thing tonight and the schoolgirl outfit is what I have chosen to wear in front of my dead boyfriend, who I stupidly dumped yesterday.

"Err, yeah, the uniform..." I mumble looking down at it again, unable to believe what I'm wearing myself now. "I've got a fancy dress party this weekend, so must have forgotten to take it off, after trying it on earlier" I add, quickly making out it was a genuine mistake.

Yeah, a genuine mistake if you're slightly crazy and planning to have a sexual fantasy with a rotting corpse in the basement tonight. Who may I add, is looking a lot more attractive and desirable the deader he gets.

"Well, I happen to think you pull off the schoolgirl stance perfectly, Jenna" Mr Harper chirps, trying to pay me a compliment.

Wow, I can't believe he bought it. Saying that, what other reason than that crazy one I've just given would he have believed otherwise?

"I'm sorry Mr Harper, I thought I took it off" I tell him. "Do you want me to run home quickly and get changed?" I ask him.

He ponders on my suggestion for a few seconds, then decides he has a better idea. As I watch him take a piece of paper from my desk, I watch him write something down.

(DRESS AS YOU PLEASE NIGHT)
Please give generously to our good cause.

Okay, I can clearly read what he's written, but I don't understand why.

"If you don't mind wearing your schoolgirl uniform tonight Jenna, then we can put it to good use" he suggests, putting the note up on the desk, with a small tin to collect money beside it.

Oh, I see what he's doing now. Wow, this guy is pretty smart, I think to myself, agreeing with his idea.

"Yeah, we can maybe put the money you raise towards a nice plaque for Christina" he then adds.

Stupid fucking idea, I hate it, I think to myself again, forcing a smile onto my face, then nodding my head in agreement anyway.

8:32pm (Friday 2nd April)

I'm so glad Mr Harper has finally gone home and I'm so pleased he didn't think I was going insane wearing what I chose to wear to work tonight. Seriously, I've got to hold it together, otherwise this crazy behavior might actually get the serial killer in me caught soon. I can't believe I let this happen. I mean, I remember having the dressing up idea for Greg before I left for work, and I remember trying this outfit on, but how I didn't put it in a bag; to change into later on is a mystery to me. What must people of thought, as I made my way to work this evening? A nineteen year old walking down the street, with a short schoolgirl skirt on, fashioning a white shirt and a pink tie – Crazy!

"Oh well" I chirp to myself, pleased that everything turned out okay in the end, then that nothing more came of it.

Wow, there were so many things worrying me before work tonight, but my dress code wasn't one of them. In all the confusion, I actually forgot to ask Mr Harper if Dean had turned up today, then whether he tried to talk himself out of the hole he dug for himself on the last shift.

Tonight this shift is going to be different. Once I've

settled the guests coming in tonight, I'm not going to worry myself about their private lives and I'm not entering the secret passageway for any reason. My killing days are well and truly behind me. In-fact, if a cheating man does come in, I'm not going to get upset with him at all. I'm simply going to do my job, figure out a way of disposing of all the bodies in the basement, then I'm going to get on with my life. After of course, Greg and I have tried out this uniform fantasy thing. Hey, what's the point in wasting an opportunity, if I'm already wearing it?

9:29pm (Friday 2nd April)

Finally, we have some guests coming in. For a minute there I thought I was going to be on my own all night long. The hotel has only ever had zero guests once before and that was only because there was a crazy lunatic waving a gun around outside. Okay, this seems like a nice enough couple coming towards me, but why is he wearing sunglasses? Who does he think he is, some kind of Hollywood star or...

"You're Bruce Wilson, aren't you?" I crazily ask, the second they're in front of me at the desk, forgetting my professional script as hotel manageress. "And you're Cameron Davis, aren't you?" I then add, spotting the famous female beside him too.

Okay, this has got to be one of those mental dreams again, hasn't it? I mean, why would two Hollywood superstars come into our hotel? We've never had a celebrity stay here before. It certainly looks like them, unless of course they are some of these celebrity look-a-likes, because we get a lot of those around these parts.

"Shh, don't tell anyone" whispers the guy who I think is Bruce Wilson.

Wow, that's certainly the best look-a-like I've ever seen, considering he sounds like the star too.

"How many guests have you got in tonight, Lovely?" the female I think is Cameron asks next.

Wow, she sounds like her celebrity double as well, doesn't she? What do I tell these guys? I can hardly tell them we're empty, if it is them.

"You're the first in tonight" I answer, deciding to go with the truth, considering that's what my mouth wanted to say before my head started getting involved in telling them a lie.

"Okay, here's what we need you to do" the Bruce Wilson look-a-like whispers next. "We need you to close the main doors and allow no-one else to check in tonight" he adds.

Yeah right, and why would I do that?

"If you do" says the Cameron look-a-like. "Then we'll pay you fifty grand for the night" she adds, showing me a little handbag full of cash.

I didn't think look-a-likes got paid this much. Wow, what if it is really them? How does a hotel receptionist turned manageress look after a couple of superstars?

"Miss..."

"MISS..."

"Oh yeah sorry, sure thing" I tell them, logging onto my computer to take their details, then asking for their names.

"I thought you already knew our names" giggles the female, as I all of a sudden feel completely starstruck.

"Miss Davis and Mr Wilson, yeah?" I utter, checking anyway.

"That's right" the real Bruce Wilson chirps. "And if you keep our little visit highly confidential, then there will be an extra personal bonus in it for you by morning" he adds, clearly trying to buy my silence and doing it so very well.

Once the two A-list celebrities are fully checked in and I hand them the key-card to room number eight upstairs; because it's the room used the least, I've really got to ask the question.

"Why have you guys decided to stay here tonight?" I ask, pointing out Manhattan is only a few blocks away.

"Isn't this where that murder took place the other day?" asks Bruce Wilson.

"Yeah, but it happened across the street, not in this actual hotel" I respond.

"Then that's why we're staying here" he answers, telling me absolutely nothing, as my face goes blank with confusion.

Luckily for me, Cameron notices this.

"No one would ever expect us to be staying in a hotel under such a huge media spotlight, so it's our perfect hideaway" she explains.

Wow, that's actually a really clever idea!

As I watch the couple walk up the staircase all smiles, I can't believe how cunning a huge celebrity must need to be to avoid well, everything. With cameras pointing in their faces all day long, of course they're going to look for an isolated place like this to enjoy their free time. Oh... I said free time, didn't I? As in free time with their families and loved ones, yet why are they here alone then? Okay, okay calm down Jenna, this visit doesn't mean anything –

They could just be looking for a little bit of peace and quiet. Yeah, it looks that way, doesn't it? That's why I'm watching them walk upstairs together and Mr Wilson clearly has his arm around Cameron's waist – The dirty lying cheats!

Okay Jenna, remember what you promised yourself – No more killing people, no more getting involved. Yeah, but it's the principle of the thing, isn't it? I mean, they've just bribed me with fifty thousand dollars, just so I will keep their obvious affair secret. I mean, how much would the tabloids pay for such a story? Double that perhaps? Even up to a million, considering how huge these two people are? How dare they humiliate me like this – How dare they think they can buy my silence with a lousy offer.

As I watch the Hollywood stars enter their room upstairs, then once that door is closed, I shut up shop, lock the main door as requested, then race towards my secret passageway upstairs too.

"Let's see what a cheating celebrity couple do behind closed doors, shall we?" I mumble to myself, climbing the stairs.

He's definitely married with children and the last I heard, she was engaged to some kind of pop star. Silly celebrities – Fancy checking into a hotel, where the manageress kills you for fornicating in such a way.

9:42pm (Friday 2nd April)

Since swiping my key-card at the secret passageway door, I've entered the walkway and had a little re-think. I mean, was I of sane mind coming into work this evening?

Was I promising not to kill anyone else? Why should it bother me, if these two want to destroy lives and cheat?

Obviously a million questions are floating around my head, as I stand looking at the hole which will show me their room, but I'm not ready to look yet. I mean, killing someone like Greg, where his family now assume he's traveling Europe is one thing, but how do you make a Hollywood star disappear? Should I even be thinking this, considering I'm not a killer any longer? But you will be if you look through that hole, won't you Jenna? Why do I kill? I mean, it's not like I could have done anything else with the likes of Greg, but surely I don't have to go this far, this time? Why not expose them? Wow, what a headline that would be. Not only would the tabloids make the accusation of the affair very public, but if I take a few pictures tonight too, I've then got the proof, haven't I? Wow, that's scary – Just think how many people will notice a story because of little old me. Millions and millions of people will be interested in something I've discovered. Almost seems too big in my own head, doesn't it? Oh how killing someone sounds a lot easier to do, when there's not a spotlight to fill.

10:02pm (Friday 2nd April)

After exactly twenty minutes of deliberation, I've finally decided to have a quick look through the hole, then I will let my mood at the time choose their fate. As my heart races, as I go out of my mind with worry, I brace myself, then take a look holding my breath.

"Oh..."

Well here's a first. The lights are out, they've clearly gone to bed and I feel I may have overreacted for the first time in my life. See Jenna, this is why you convinced yourself not to kill anybody else, because you clearly get things wrong. Just like you did with Mr Bentley last night, you might have killed this innocent famous couple, then regretted it later on. Think before you act Jenna. Remember, no one else needs to die.

10:05pm (Friday 2nd April)

Feeling slightly ashamed of myself for judging too soon, I leave the passageway with my tail between my legs, tempting myself to jump over the banister, so the fall into the reception area will kill me. Deciding that's what I've got to do to end this crazy behavior, I take another deep breath, then head towards it, thinking about my Greg.

WHAT THE FUCK?

Those dirty celebrity assholes are at it on top of my brand-new desk. Look at Bruce standing upright, pinning Cameron's body and open legs against my computer screen. Fucking celebrities think they rule the world, don't they? Think Jenna, think. What do you want to do about this? Kill them both, right now, that's what. No wait, wait... Think it through properly first.

"Oh yeah, yeah, oh yeah" cries Cameron, knocking my monitor over with her huge naked ass, as he continues to thrust at her.

How dare they have sex on my desk – How dare they cheat on their loved ones like this – More importantly, just remembering it now, how dare they not notice the schoolgirl outfit I have on right now and not tell me how pretty I look.

"I hate them, I hate them, I hate them" I grunt under my breath, pacing the upstairs landing, trying to blank out what they're doing to my lovely work station.

Wanting to growl at them, still very much wanting to kill them both, I decide the best thing to do is pull my phone out and start snapping pictures.

"Fifty grand? I'll show you what you can do with your fifty grand offer" I huff, clicking, pointing and snapping as many as I can. "Ooh yeah, that was a good shot Cameron" I giggle, claiming I have them just where I want them now.

With that I head back to the staircase, then start my subtle descent. Still clicking at the bottom, the arrogant couple don't even notice when I'm almost standing beside them, then they hear my camera click.

"What the fuck do you think you're doing?" growls Cameron, leaping off the desk, where I continue to snap, getting a good few shots of their private parts together too.

"I think you should stop taking pictures of us and hand me the phone right now" Bruce angrily suggests.

"Why, what are you going to do about it?" I immediately ask. "You're not an action hero in real life. You can't just pull out a gun and shoot me" I remind him, as though the asshole needs reminding.

"What are you planning to do with those photos, Lovely?" she then asks, putting her clothes back on in the process.

Oh... I haven't thought this far ahead, have I?

"A lot more than your pathetic fifty grand was going to do" I growl at her.

"So, you want money, do you?" she asks.

Wow, isn't she smart working that out all by herself? Hold on... Is she? Is that what I'm doing here? Have I suddenly turned from serial killer into a blackmailer now then? MM-mm, I wonder what I could do with a few thousand dollars?

"A cool million and you hand over the phone" she suggests, knocking me sideways a little bit with her very generous offer.

Wow, I was thinking about a few thousand dollars, but I'm sure she's just offered me a million. I think I might be a little out of my comfort zone here, considering I can't imagine what these pictures are actually worth. MM-mm yeah, a million dollars - I could do plenty with that – Like leave the country and never get caught – Like start my life somewhere else and...

"Well?" she calls out.

"Two million and I will give you my phone" I instantly respond, happy with the one million offer a few seconds ago, but not now the rude bitch has cut my thinking short.

"Okay then, two million dollars. Hand over the phone then" she demands, holding out her hand to receive it.

"What do you think I am Bitch, some little girl straight out of school?" I huff at her, clearly realizing the hypocrisy, considering I'm standing here in my schoolgirl uniform. "You two go and find the money for me now, then I will hand my phone over later" I tell her.

Wow, I can be quite firm when I want to be, can't I?

"I will stay here with you, if it's all the same" she quickly responds, claiming she wouldn't want to turn her back on me, considering I might copy the pictures.

Wow, she is a smart cookie, isn't she? Because I would have never thought of that either!

10:23pm (Friday 2nd April)

The famous action hero Bruce Wilson left the hotel a few minutes ago and here I sit at my desk with Cameron Davis on the seats in front of me, waiting for his return.

"So, considering you're so young, at what age did you get yourself into blackmailing people?" she huffs at me, not even decent enough to look my way when she's speaking to me.

"Believe it or not, this is my first time" I tell her, knowing she isn't going to bitch talk her way out of this one tonight.

"Why, what did you do before that, prostitution?" she responds, looking me and my schoolgirl outfit up and down, as if I was a piece of dirt.

"No actually, I started out as a serial killer" I bitch back at her, determined to not let her have the final say. This doesn't worry her as she sits there playing with her celebrity fake nails like a diva.

"So, what are you going to do with your well earned two mill, Honey?" she asks, as though I haven't earned the right to make this kind of money myself, but she has dancing around on the silver screen like she does.

"Open up a print shop, start up a magazine, then expose whore's like you" I respond, deciding to up the anti every time she lowers the tone.

"Wow, you are one messed up little girl, aren't you?" she then responds, which secretly boils my blood like it's never been boiled before.

"Say, would you mind helping me lift something out of the basement?" I ask in a friendly manner, wanting to rip her head off right fucking now!

"No, you're okay, Honey" she responds, looking at me as though she wouldn't lift a finger to help anyone anyway.

"How about you come over to Jentina and have a drink with me then?" I ask, trying to tempt her another way.

"What, drink and put on weight, I don't think so"

What do I have to do to get this horrible celebrity bitch down into the basement?

"I've got a little bit of work to do, so I will be back in a few minutes. I will be in the basement if you need me" I sing out, standing up.

"If you want that two million dollars Babes, then that camera doesn't leave my sight, so shut up, sit down and..."

Fuck this...

"I'M GOING TO COPY EVERY SINGLE PICTURE ON MY PHONE RIGHT NOW!" I yell, sprinting for the basement door as quickly as I can, knowing she's got to follow me now.

"Come back here you little whore" she instantly calls out, falling straight into my trap – The trap I'm clearly making up, as I run.

I open the basement door, making sure it's left open for her to follow. I then race downstairs and quickly hide in the dark, completely out of sight.

"Seriously you little bitch, this isn't funny. I want that camera in my sight the whole time" she calls out, clearly sounding nervous about the dark, as she creeps down the stairs towards me.

As soon as her feet are in front of me, I reach through the gap in between the steps and pull against her leg as hard as I can. Her screams are pathetic and to be perfectly honest, I thought an actress would be able to fall down the stairs a lot more convincing than this. First I consider jumping out, switching on the lights, then talking to her. Then I think about giving her a chance to save her own life. Then finally I decide to...

"Die you horrible cheating whore, die. Die, so I never have to see your ugly cheating face on the television ever again" I scream, obviously stabbing her to death.

I do the utmost of craziest of things sometimes, don't I? I mean, fancy stabbing her to death down here, knowing she can't stay down here after she's dead. It's not like the other guys in the room are going to behave once I've left, are they? This is Cameron Davis we're talking about after all, not just some random woman. Cameron Davis who I think locked in a room with four men would certainly get gang raped. Oh look at that – It's happening already, isn't it?

"No Mr Sullivan, you can't lie on top of her like that. She's a celebrity, not a piece of meat" I huff, telling Mr Sullivan off for diving on top of her dying body, as I nearly break my back trying to lift him on top of her myself.

"What was that Greg? You'd like to finger her?" I ask Greg, who's eyes although still open, clearly light up the room.

Or was that me just switching on the light down here?

"Greg, you're a cheat, a liar and a dirty bastard, but I love you" I tell him, knocking his sitting up body to the side, so he falls over beside her. "Then because I love you so much, I'm going to talk Cameron into letting you do this to her" I add, quickly unbuttoning her jeans, then placing Greg's hand inside her knickers.

Wow, it's like playing with life sized dolls, isn't it?

"Watch your fingers Greg, your hands are very cold" I playfully warn him, placing his ice cold fingers against Cameron's still warm pubic area.

With that, I casually walk over to the light, switch it off, then back on again.

"GREG YOU CHEATING ASSHOLE!" I yell out, furious at him for doing this to me. "You want to finger a cheating tart, then watch me kill her" I scream, grabbing Cameron by the hair and dragging her back towards the stairs.

"I will teach you to let my boyfriend touch you!" I scream at her dead body.

Step by step I start to pull her upwards.

"Watch your head Cameron" I laugh, using all my energy to pull her up the stairs by her hair, watching as her head whacks against every single step with joy.

As we reach the top, I open the door and drag her motionless body into reception, where a trail of blood follows her twitching corpse.

"Wow, you're pretty good at this dying thing, aren't you Cameron? Have you ever played a stiff before?" I ask her, yet she strangely doesn't respond.

Whilst the trail of blood gets longer and longer, I decide she can't die in this hotel, because Bruce knows she's here, so I drag her to the main entrance. As I pick her lifeless body up, then open the door with my other hand, the bitch has covered me in her nasty blood, so I get really angry with her now.

"Get out and stay out!" I huff at her, tossing her body out onto the street, as though I care any longer.

Shit... Somebody is going to find her, aren't they? Quickly

Jenna, think. Take her phone out of her pocket, so no-one will be able to identify her at least.

Leaving a famous dead person out on the street might not be one of my better ideas and worse still, this time I don't even have a plan. Saying that, this is her phone, isn't it? So surely she must... Yes she does, she has Bruce Wilson's number right here, look...

I call Bruce Wilson pressing my blood stained fingers all over the screen, then wait for him to answer.

"Cameron, are you okay? Did you get the phone off that crazy little bitch?" he asks, answering his phone the other end.

That wasn't very nice of him to say, was it?

"No this isn't Cameron, Mr Dick" I respond. "Cameron ran off and left the hotel, so it's down to you to pay me for these pictures now" I tell him.

"If she's not there, then how have you got her phone?" he suddenly asks me.

Err... Damn it – This is why you must always think up a plan before acting it out Jenna.

"Err... She dropped it when she ran off" I tell him, thinking of the first thing that enters my head.

Suddenly the conversion over the phone turns to business again, once he believes my fictional story.

"Look Miss Crazy, I can't get my hands on that kind of money at this time of night" he tells me.

"Fine, how much can you get then?" I growl at him, trying to work out how much this next offer is going to be dropped from the initial two million dollar offer.

"One and a half" he says. "I've managed to lay my hands on one and a half million" he adds, clearly hoping I will accept it.

Considering I didn't want any money in the first place, then only expected a few thousand for my troubles, yeah I can do this amount no problem. I tell him where to meet me, warn him that he must turn up alone, then for some strange reason thank him for his generous offer.

With the new plan, which isn't exactly clear in my own mind yet, I leave the hotel and plan to head towards the little park I've asked to meet him in.

"Get out the way Cameron, you're blocking my way" I huff at the dead celebrity still on the pavement, before casually dragging her sorry ass back inside again and out of the way. "You wait here, whilst I go and pick up my money" I tell her, making sure I also tell her that I love her lacy knickers, because she hasn't done her jeans back up after Greg fingering her.

Ready to leave, ready to pick up my money, then ready to fly off to Mexico or somewhere straight after, I don't leave the hotel after all. I can hardly walk down the road in this state, can I? I step back inside once more; knowing there are some new uniforms hanging up in room five, then kick Cameron in the ribs for fucking up my schoolgirl outfit with her nasty blood.

CHAPTER 12 – *NEWS*

It's been a whole hour since I rang Bruce Wilson and another ten minutes waiting here in this dark park alone.

"Any longer Bruce and I'm afraid you're going to end up like Cameron too" I whisper to myself, making sure my trusty knife is concealed down the back of my trousers.

1.02 am (Saturday 3rd April)

"I thought you weren't going to show up" I sing out, noticing Mr Wilson finally come towards me in the dark, only three minutes later.

"Although I don't agree with blackmail, I do believe a blackmailer can be silenced, so I'm sure this matter is done and dusted with now" he responds, handing me the bag full of cash, requesting I now hand over the phone.

I hand him my phone, my trusty phone, that I've had for a

few years now, but once I've looked into the bag full of notes, I feel happy enough realizing it can be replaced. I only had Christina's name on my contacts list anyway and I don't suppose she's going to ring me any time soon.

"So, are we done here then?" he asks, putting my phone in his jacket pocket for safe keeping.

"Not quite, Mr Bruce" I answer, knowing I've got one final thing I want to say, before he flutters off back to Hollywood.

I tell him that the exchange we've just made was fair enough, but that isn't the end of the deal. I inform him I want him to take at least a year long holiday from public view and he's not to emerge again under any circumstances whatsoever.

"You've made copies of the photos, haven't you? Do you realize how many people I know? And how many of those people would make you disappear at the sound of my voice?" he threatens.

Everything goes eerily silent, as I weigh up what he's just said to me.

"Well?" he then barks at me in the dark, like a stray dog without a home to go to.

"Oh yeah, sorry Mr Wilson. It was just hearing you threaten my like that, made me think I was in one of your great movies" I laugh at him, before putting my serious face back on. "One year gone and no, I haven't copied the photos" I tell him, claiming that would have been really dishonest of me.

"If this deal is done, then why would I let you destroy my career for a whole year too?" he laughs.

"The photo's wouldn't destroy you Mr Wilson, but the text messages on Cameron's phone I've now got in my possession certainly would" I laugh back at him, demanding he leave me alone now.

Mugged, robbed and blackmailed, Mr Bruce Wilson knows I have him over a barrel and there's nothing he can do about it, if he doesn't want his little Cameron secret out.

"Oh and Mr Wilson" I call out, as he stops to listen to his new master, me. "Come back here and sign your autograph on my bra, will you? I'm a huge fan"

1:41 am (Saturday 3rd April)

With a bag full of cash, a new uniform on and a way out of this mess at last, I weigh up my options heading back in the direction of the hotel. I can either leave now and be happy for the rest of my life, or head back, clean up and carry on as normal, but which one is right for me?

Everything points me in the direction of leaving and setting up somewhere new, except one thing – Greg. I can't possibly leave him down in that basement on his side like that. I can't leave without washing the cheap celebrity scent off his fingers, before I go. I just want to see his beautiful dead face one last time, before this all ends. I have to go back, don't I?

7:51 am (Saturday 3rd April)

"Morning Jenna, how was your night?" Mr Harper asks, entering the building.

"Wonderful" I answer, claiming we've been packed out and I've even managed to clean and sparkle up the reception floor - For obviously red strained reasons of course, but he doesn't know this.

"And you even managed to find a uniform and seemingly check everyone out before seven" he sings, looking at the guest list on my computer screen, which I've had hours to adjust.

"That's not the only good news" I sing out, not wanting him to be pleased with me, but really pleased with me. "When I was wearing my schoolgirl uniform, I took a donation of two thousand dollars" I tell him, handing the cash straight over, which I've obviously placed in the tin myself.

"Wow Jenna, I mean wow. You know what? Christina would be so proud of you right now" he sings out.

"That's not the best news either, Mr Harper" I add, wanting this to keep going for as long as I can. "A guest last night also left me a personal thousand dollar tip and the hotel twenty-five thousand" I continue.

Okay Mr Harper, I wanted you to be happy, not cry. Come on, take it, take the money. Lay your hands on Mr Wilson's dirty cheating cash too.

"Oh Jenna, you're such a wonderful employee" he sings, clearly overjoyed.

"Manageress Mr Harper, I'm your manageress" I laugh with him, heading for the weekend and the main entrance I think I deserve.

"Have a wonderful break Jenna" he calls out.

And there is it, the appreciation I've always dreamed of receiving working here.

"Oh and Mr Harper" I call back. "I've also set up a guy to come in on Wednesday to clear the basement out and replace the door" I add, obviously needing him to stay away from it for the next two days, because Cameron did eventually have to join the boys down there.

With one deliriously happy boss and me feeling on top of the world; as well as rich, I exit the building knowing the weekend couldn't have come at a better time. I've got money to burn, I've got plans to make, so this next couple of days is going to be... Oh no, what's this? Why the hell is that Dean guy back inside his bar, staring at me through the window? Why does he look like he's been sitting there all night long and now he's shaking his head in my direction? He watched me throw Cameron Davis onto the street earlier, didn't he? He knows everything, doesn't he? Quickly Jenna, get over there and kill him, before he tells on you.

As my slow and casual walk towards him fills my heart with fear, I desperately try to keep that fear from my face, as he unlocks his door in front of me. Come on then Disco Dean, tell me what you saw? Don't hold out on me?

"I think we need a little chat, don't you?" he grumbles at me, giving me the sign to enter his little establishment. Taking a seat at the bar seems to be the easiest part, then waiting for him to walk around to the other side, seems to be the hardest. Come on Dean, tell me what you know. If I've got to kill you, then I'd much rather do it before the sun comes up fully.

"Drink?" he chirps, reaching the other side of the bar. "Oh that's right Jenna, you don't drink, do you?" he adds, with a hint of scary sarcasm in his voice.

Seriously Dean, get to your point, because I haven't come this far or earned a bag full of cash to be stopped by someone like you.

"Why did you purposely set me up with that woman the other day? Why did you purposely get me fired?" he then starts the questions rolling.

Play dumb Jenna, he can't prove a thing.

"I've been sitting here for at least an hour now and it's clear you wanted me out of the hotel before I even started" he grunts at me.

Did he just say an hour? That means he saw nothing of the Cameron incident, did he?

"Look Dean, I'm sorry" I say, standing up ready to leave again. "But if you haven't noticed, my friend Christina died a few days ago, so I haven't been myself lately" I explain, so he understands.

"But you purposely got me fired" he huffs again, as though he isn't going to do anything about it, other than sulk.

I've just taken on two Hollywood's superstars and won, so you're hardly any match for me Deano.

"What would you like me to do, to put it right?" I ask, deliberately looking as though I need to leave very soon.

"I want my life back. I want my business back" he grunts my way, as though it's not possible for him to see it happening himself.

"Okay then, let me do that for you" I announce, unfazed by his gritted teeth, angry face routine.

"What?" he shudders, finally hearing what I've just said.

"I will have Jentina closed down by Monday and turned into a cinema or something else" I tell him. "I will then GIVE you the money to build your business again, making it even better than it was before" I add.

"Don't you mean lend me the money? Why, where are you going to get around fifty grand from?" he asks, slightly skeptical about my offer.

Once I've told him about my make-believe rich cousin and assured him I'm giving him the money, not lending him it, it's a done deal.

"Why would you give me the money?" he asks.

Okay, I thought it was a done deal.

"As you pointed out, I've done you wrong Dean. I can't change the fact I was upset about my friend CHRISTINA, but I can do this for you, so you won't hate me" I explain.

"Hate you? I will absolutely love you if you're serious" he beams, finally getting excited about my freebie offer.

"How does two hundred grand sound?" I ask him.

"That sounds a little too much" he responds, shocked by my generous offer.

"Two hundred grand to start up your business, not tell a soul where you got the money from and I will drop it around later on today in cash" I tell him, holding out my hand to shake his and hopefully seal the deal.

10:32 am (Saturday 3rd April)

As I arrive home absolutely exhausted, knowing this weekend's rest is well and truly needed, I'm feeling on top of the world. I've killed off a few bad guys – I'm going to have Mr Harper eating out of the palm of hand from now on – And to top it off, Disco Dean has forgiven me too. All in all, despite the rudeness of the Hollywood asshole's, it's been a wonderful shift at the Cure Hotel.

Time for me to switch on the TV and relax, then head back to Dean's bar with that money I promised him later on this afternoon.

Breaking news... It is feared that Hollywood superstar Cameron Davis has been murdered.

Oh dear, this wasn't supposed to happen, was it?

After a tip off about a blood stain outside a hotel this morning, it has been confirmed that the blood is that of Miss Davis, although her body hasn't yet been discovered.

"Fucking hell. They're going to search the basement, aren't they?" I grumble, feeling the need to get back to the hotel fast.

The number one suspect at the moment is fellow Hollywood actor Bruce Wilson. His name has been linked to the disappearance of Miss Davis, because her phone records have suggested the couple were having an affair. Mr Wilson hasn't been located at this time.

Wow, what do I do with her phone now then? I only held onto it because I needed it. If the police have discovered details of the affair through phone records, then there's no need for Bruce Wilson to keep me out of it, is there? Shit... They are definitely going to search the hotel, aren't they? They're definitely going to raid the basement. This could be it Jenna, the moment where you're found out. Should I flea now? Should I head down to the hotel to find out what's going on? Oh no, Greg, I haven't said goodbye to him yet.

11:25am (Saturday 3ʳᵈ April) – (My day off)

Although I haven't slept in hours, my adrenaline is working overtime as I arrive back at the hotel to complete carnage. Worse than it was when Christina was murdered, police presence has tripled here this morning and the whole street has been cordoned off.

"Excuse me officer, but can I come through?" I call out, being held back by the police, tape and photographers out in their hundreds.

"No one is allowed past the tape Miss" he growls.

"But I work in that hotel. I was working there last night. I checked Bruce Wilson and Cameron Davis in" I tell him.

I have no idea why I just said this and have no idea why all the cameras are now flashing at me, but I'm glad he's seen sense and is now guiding me towards the hotel, as though he's my bodyguard.

As I walk into the building the place is packed again, but this time, the downstairs rooms are clearly being searched and the place is being tipped upside down.

"JENNA, JENNA" calls Mr Harper through the crowds of people, waving me over. "Did you know Bruce Wilson and Cameron Davis were staying here last night?" he asks.

"Yes I do Mr Harper. They are the ones that left the huge tip" I announce, as everyone around me listens.

"But there's no record of them staying here on the computer" calls another officer, standing at my computer, obviously ripping that apart too.

"They didn't want their real names used" I respond, instantly telling him they went under the name Mr and Mrs Jones.

"Room five boys. Upstairs now" calls the officer behind the desk, finding the information on the screen he finally needs.

Now, once they've found what I left for them to find in room five, this should end the search and keep my basement out of bounds pretty quickly.

"MISS... MISS..." calls another officer from the banister. "Did you enter this room, after they checked out?" he asks.

"No, I went home. It was the end of my shift" I call back, as he then calls the detective standing with us, up to the room urgently.

Wow, I wonder what they've found?

11:38am (Saturday 3rd April)

Once six hundred or so officers, doctors, scientists and god knows who else have been up and down the stairs for ten minutes, the detective returns to Mr Harper and I, sitting in the reception area.

"So what's going on, have you found her?" Mr Harper asks, worried like hell about the situation and his hotel's reputation.

You can't blame him really can you? I mean, all this hard work to turn this place into a beautiful hotel and the police are ripping it apart.

"A lot of blood has been found in the bathroom, but no body" the detective responds. "Looks like whatever happened up there last night, wasn't a pleasant outcome for someone" he adds.

Okay, and this is my cue to breakdown and start crying again. Ready? Go.

"It's okay Jenna, it's okay" Mr Harper instantly comforts me, claiming he knows this must be hard on me, consider I was working when it all happened.

Oh good – Everyone pay attention, because I'm the victim here, not the killer. Oh how I love turning the water-works on and fooling everyone in the process.

"Search this hotel from top to bottom and find me that body" the detective calls out, as I freak out and start to cry for real this time.

No, no, no, no, no they found the room, so get out. Go and find Bruce Wilson and search his house instead, there's no body to be found here. Oh my god, this is it, isn't it? I'm going to get caught for sure now?

"Move, move, I'm going to be sick" I freak out, pushing people out of the way, in a bid to make my escape at the main entrance.

"Sorry Miss Cole, but we can't let you leave now. You're going to have to be sick in a bin or something" says another officer grabbing hold of me.

What? How can they keep me here, when I walked in of my own accord? Shall I be sick, just for the sake of it? I certainly feel a little sick now.

12:02pm (Saturday 3rd April) – (Still my day off)

"Detective, we've found something over here" calls another random officer, as Mr Harper and I can only watch them tear the hotel to shreds as they emerge from the downstairs passageway.

Her body isn't in there, so what could they have possibly found?

The detective disappears straight away, then returns a couple of minutes later.

"Mr Harper, can you tell me if anyone uses that passageway whilst the hotel is open?" he asks.

"Not that I know of" Mr Harper responds, looking at me as though I might know any different.

"It's just we've found a few spy-holes leading into every room, so just wanted to know if you knew about them?" the detective continues to probe.

Suddenly Mr Harper catches on.

"Oh you mean the little holes about five centimeters round?" he responds. "Yeah, those are where I plan to put the control pads for the rooms" he adds, all smiles about this idea.

"Fine Mr Harper, but has anyone ever used those holes to spy on your visitors?" the detective asks.

"ABSOLUTELY NOT!" Mr Harper barks, horrified at such a suggestion, once we're told to follow the detective into the passageway, so I grab Mr Harper's arm quickly.

"Christina used to take her breaks in there all the time" I whisper to him, so he isn't in the dark about what I think the police are going to suggest next.

As we enter the narrow walkway with one officer and the detective, we arrive at the very first hole.

"Are you telling me these holes are for electrical purposes only?" the detective asks.

"They sure are" Mr Harper responds, showing them how the control pad is going to work from this side of the wall.

"And you made these holes in the wall, did you Sir?" the detective asks, working his way towards the point he's trying to make.

"Of course I did. I've been building most of this hotel alone for ages" Mr Harper answers.

"Then can you tell me why these hand prints have been found at every hole, if no-one has used them to spy on people?"

There you go – There's Mr Harper's shock and silence.

Look at him trying to work it out, then look at me for the answers again.

"Did you know anything about these holes, Miss Cole?" the officer then asks me.

"Me? I didn't even know this room existed until now" I answer, remembering what Christina must have felt last week when she discovered it.

"I'm sorry Mr Harper, but because you placed the holes here and there's clear evidence the holes have been used for sinister purposes, I'm going to have to arrest you" says the detective, reading my boss his rights.

Wow, I'm glad I didn't discover this narrow passageway until now, otherwise that could be me getting arrested and handcuffed.

"Jenna, when they've finished here, lock up and keep the place ticking over for me" Mr Harper calls out, throwing me his main door key, before being led away.

Is this a good time to remind him that it's still my weekend off?

"Okay Miss Cole, where shall we search next?" the detective then questions me. "How about the basement?" he suggests.

Maybe I should have let them arrest me for the holes, considering the basement is going to freak them out and Mr Harper can't be blamed now. Or can he?

"Have you got the key, Miss Cole?" he asks, thinking I've just been handed them by Mr Harper.

Here we go then.

"No, this door hasn't been opened since Mr Harper took over the place" I tell him. "Mr Harper is always saying that he will get round to fixing it, but he never does" I add.

Sorry Mr Harper, but from now on in, it's everyone for

themselves, I'm afraid.

Come on Mr Policeman Sir, let's leave this door, shall we? You've already found the blood upstairs, so what more do you want, her body too?

"Do you find something funny, Miss Cole?" the detective questions me, noticing I'm giggling nervously for some reason.

"No" I answer, instantly dropping my head, fearing this door being opened more than anything else in the whole world, then nervously giggling about it again.

12:26pm (Saturday 3rd April)

"Okay lads, break it down" the detective gives the order, as I clench and hold my breath.

CHAPTER 13 – *BREAK IT DOWN*

Is this the moment in my life where I'm forced to regret everything I've ever done? Is this the moment in my life, where I'm about to pay for all my sinful acts? Not that I think they're sinful, when I've only been getting rid of the sinful sinners!

Oh well, maybe not then, considering that's the second officer who has tried to kick down the basement door, yet failed. Things might in-fact still go my way.

"Move out of the way" the detective yells. "I will do it myself" he adds, lining up for his charge at the door too. Wouldn't it be funny, if you couldn't do it either, Mr Macho asshole?

"Miss Cole, you're still laughing about something. Would you like to tell me what the joke is now?" he barks at me, claiming if there's no reason for me to laugh, then I should stop doing it.

Am I? Was I? Who knew?

Suddenly, my slight snigger turns into a full forced laugh, as he manages to kick the door off its hinges and my heart skips a few dozen beats.

"After you Miss Cole" he says with a big grin on his face, because he knows it's just stopped me giggling now.

"No way. I'm not going down there. I'm scared of the dark" I deliriously decide to freak out, knowing this is my final attempt to remain innocent.

See, if they think I'm scared of the basement, then there's no chance I'd be the one hiding all the bodies down there, would I?

"Pervis, you go first. I will hold Miss Cole's hand" the detective says, ordering his junior to go down first.

Okay Jenna, this is it. As soon as you see the bodies, scream the place down, because that's what someone innocent would... Oh, I'm going to scream now, am I?

"MISS COLE... MISS COLE, CALM YOURSELF DOWN" grunts the deafened detective, as I throw a complete and utter wobbly. "Pervis, get down there and see what you can find" he gives the next order claiming he will stay here with me after all.

Okay, that worked, I think. Now what do I do next, scream again when this Pervis finds the bodies? No, surely that would make me look silly?

Come on Pervis you penis, come on. This wait is killing me - Pardon the expression.

"All clear down here in the basement, Sir" Pervis calls out, as I start screaming the place down, then realize a few seconds later what he just said, so fall completely silent again.

I definitely left Greg sitting on the floor, when I made him finger Cameron Davis, didn't I? I definitely sat her at the bottom of the stairs, because I ran out of time to hide her body, didn't I? So how the fuck can he claim it's all clear down there?

"You've clearly been working all night and are very tired, Miss Cole" the detective says to me, after my latest screaming fit dies down. "I think you should go home, get some rest, because this is clearly an emotional time for you" he adds.

Aha, isn't that nice – He is considerate after all the shouting and ordering about he does. HOLD ON... Where are the bodies then? Where's my Greg? Seriously, if these guys weren't all standing around me right now, I'd be down in the basement searching for him myself.

Okay Jenna, Okay... Like he said, I'm clearly very emotional and tired, so relax and think back. What the hell did you do with the bodies earlier on this morning? Oh that's right...

"What's right?" the detective asks me.

Shit, did I just say that out loud? Wow, I must be tired, considering I can't control my own secret thoughts now.

"Nothing" I tell him, agreeing with his last comment about me being tired.

And now saying and thinking the word tired, I let out my first huge yawn. GOT IT, I know where the bodies are... Shh brain, don't say this part out loud too. I did take those bodies out, didn't I? I told Mr Harper a man was coming in to clean out the basement on Wednesday, but I got him to do it this morning instead, didn't I? Yeah, that's right – I'm not going insane.

6:41pm (Saturday 3rd April)

"Jenna. Wake up"

"J... J... Jen... Jenna, w... wake u... up"

Oh fuck not another nightmare about Mr Hodge. Wow, I really need this now, don't I? Okay, where did all the police go? Why have I just woken up in the reception seating area alone like this?

"Where is everyone?" I grumble, trying to open my eyes wide enough to see.

"T... they... they're all d... d... dead" Mr Hodge suddenly sniggers like a crazy man, standing over me.

OKAY, OKAY, it must be a dream, so go with it and relax.

"What are you doing Mr Hodge? What are you doing here?" I ask, not worried about this freaky occurrence now I know I'm not awake.

As I sit up, as I try to move away, he then swings a chair with full force pinning me against the seating area with it.

OKAY, OKAY, It's not a dream, it's not a dream!

"Please Mr Hodge, what are you doing?" I scream, ready to cry for real.

"I... I've... I've come to tell y... you what a b... b... bad girl you've b... b... been" he stutters, like the creepy old man he is.

"Okay, okay, you've told me, I get it, I'm bad. Now get this chair off me" I demand, struggling to free up my trapped arms.

"O... okay then... but o... only once I've k... k... killed you" he responds, pulling my trusty knife out from behind his back, freaking me out even more. "I... I told you, I... I watched you" he adds, licking the blade.

Although I can't think straight because I've just woken up and can't digest anything he's saying either, I do know that this isn't a dream, because the chair is pinching my arm so much, it's actually hurting.

"Get the fuck off me!" I growl again, finally overpowering him, freeing up one of my legs, then kicking him where it should hurt.

"You can r... run J... Jenna, but you can't h... hide" he calls out, slowly picking himself up off the floor, as I sprint for the main entrance.

Great, it's fucking locked. Okay, you disgusting old man, let's do this. If you want to take me on, come on and try!

I pick up one of the many new plant pots sitting around the reception area and wave it in his direction.

"I don't know what your problem is Mr Hodge, but you'd better leave me alone" I threaten, aiming the pot at him, then throwing it anyway.

It hits him perfectly in the chest, but like the zombie he is, it doesn't even knock him off balance. As I watch him stagger toward me, I know I've got nothing left to throw at him, so decide to make a dash for the staircase. I know he's going to struggle to get up there in his condition, so it should give me a little time to think straight.

As I reach the top and take a breather, I know I've got to think up a plan fast, noticing he's picked up my knife again. Then I freak out completely.

"Come here you fucking whore!" he yells, strangely losing his stutter. "Come and take your punishment for killing all those people, or I'm going to fucking rip your heart out" he growls, losing his stutter again.

Was he faking his stutter all this time then? Where the

hell did the police go? Why leave me in here alone, so he could clearly walk in and do this to me?

If I thought that his stutter disappearing was a miracle of some kind, I'm then horrified when I look downstairs at him again, then try to work out how long it's going to take him to reach me, considering he can barely walk.

"Last chance Jenna. Make your confession, or die" he calls out.

"FUCK YOU, FREAK!" I scream at him.

Suddenly I find myself screaming for real, as the man with the famous limp starts sprinting up the stairs like a trained athlete.

Knowing I'm dealing with an absolute maniac now, I head towards the furthest room possible, hoping that locking myself inside will save my life. I take my key-card out of my pocket, swipe the door as quickly as I can, then make it inside just seconds before he can grab hold of my leg.

"Please leave me alone, please leave me alone" I cry out, as I place my head on the door, which he's kicking on the other side.

Knowing I'm now trapped inside a room; where if he gets in I'm finished, I slowly turn around to find a weapon to use against him, then...

"OH FUCK... NO... NO!" I scream out again, noticing Greg, Cameron and the rest of the dead gang all naked in bed together doing strange rude things to each-other, as the door comes crashing in.

"Ready to join your friends little orgy, Jenna?" Mr Hodge sniggers, knowing he has me cornered in a room, he obviously set up for me to find.

CHAPTER 14 – *THE CURE HOTEL*

Unable to look at the smile Mr Hodge has obviously stuck on all the deceased faces, I know I'm about to join them. Maybe it's karma, maybe he was the crazy one all this time, but I don't see a way out of here now, unless of course...

"Mr Hodge, I've got a bag of money stashed at home. How about I offer you a million dollars not to do this?" I plead, hoping he likes this deal better.

"What, you mean this bag?" he responds, pulling my bag from behind his back, doing his evil laugh in front of me again.

"How... how... how did you... you get into my apartment?" I question him, hating the fact he might have been inside my home without my permission.

"Careful Jenna. You're stuttering like I used to d... d... do" he mocks, before explaining it to me. "One night when you and Christina were asleep, I stole your keys and had them copied" he explains.

"So you've been in my apartment before then?" I question, feeling absolutely sick.

"Where do you think I went, when you two whores didn't let me stay here at the hotel?" he answers, instantly claiming my bed wasn't as comfortable as Christina's was, especially when he climbed into the bed with her during the day, whilst sniffing his perverse fingers saying it.

If I wasn't feeling sick already, I certainly am now!

Okay, he's got the money, he knows everything about the murders and he wants to kill me. What's the next plan Jenna? I haven't got one, have I? Move over Greg, it looks like I'm going to be joining you in the next few minutes. Hey, at least I won't be blamed for all these murders, if I'm murdered myself.

As I watch him come towards me, holding the knife ready to strike, I close my eyes, crouch down and brace for impact. Then for some reason I'm still alive sixty seconds later, yet I fear Mr Hodge is now urinating all over my head instead. That's not urine I can smell, is it? No, that's gas!

"Oh no, please Mr Hodge, not like this, please" I plead, opening my eyes, falling backwards onto the floor, watching him pour a bottle of fuel all over my body. He's going to burn me with the others, isn't he?

Although I've strangely chosen to be stabbed to death over being burnt alive, something in me tells me I'm not going to die like this. Then heaven knows why, as Mr Hodge sparks his lighter ready to kill me, a huge metal pole comes spearing through his body. I hyperventilate and star to crawl backwards, I'm then amazed to find Mr Harper standing behind him, making sure he's killed him. Instant alleviation fills my body – Instant relief shudders through my bones – Then strange joy overcomes me, knowing that Mr Hodge can now be blamed for all these murders and I can get my life back.

"Thank you Mr Harper, thank you" I leap up, wrapping my arms around the only man that's ever appreciated or cared about my feelings.

"You're quite welcome, I think" Mr Harper responds, clearly shocked himself, as our stories unfold together for the next police report.

7:32pm (Saturday 3rd April)

"Jenna, can I ask you a question?" he asks, guiding me out of the room and onto the landing. "Why the fuck are you at work, if you're not working tonight?" he asks, breaking the ice with a lame joke, which strangely comforts me so much, I hug him again beside the banister.

"Jenna, can I ask you another question?"

"Sure Mr Harper, anything" I respond, wiping the tears away from my face, because they are no longer required and this is all now over.

"Why did you kill all these people?"
Just when I thought things were going to turn out fine, this question hits me in the face like a rock, as I quickly back away from him towards the top of the staircase.

"Because my stupid boyfriend cheated on me" I answer him, still heading towards the top of the stairs, realizing he deserves to hear the truth, because he saved my terrible life just then.

"And that's reason to kill someone, is it?" he asks, remaining at the banister, clearly at arms length for the disgusting murderer I've become.

Suddenly I feel my heart breaking, as I need to explain it to him, yet I don't know how.

"Come on Jenna. Tell me why you did it" he says, clearly trusting me enough to come and sit at the top of the stairs with me, knowing I'm definitely capable of throwing him down them.

"I caught Greg and Christina cheating in one of the rooms one night" I tell him, starting to sob a little. "I have never felt pain like it in my life" I add, starting to cry, feeling that pain instantly returning to my body.

"So you thought you'd get revenge on them, did you?" he asks, trying his best to understand and follow.

"No... No, it wasn't like that at all" I assure him, clearing my throat, then wiping my eyes again. "Whilst the pain made me feel sick, I started to masturbate and enjoy it too" I tell him.

"What you were watching caused you pain, but you still sexually enjoyed it nevertheless?" he asks, trying to make sure he's got it right.

"Yeah, crazy right?" I respond, confirming that's the gist of it and that's what has made do all this.

"And what would you feel right now, if I told you it's a common emotion to feel and in certain situations, everyone feels the same?" he asks.

"I'd say you're crazier than me, Mr Harper" I respond, laughing a little about it, because the game is finally up for me and I'm well and truly caught.

"It's true Jenna, you didn't go insane, you aren't a crazy killer. You just didn't know how to deal with a common emotion a lot of people will face in their lives" he tells me.

"But how can something so painful, turn you on?" I ask, doubting every last word he's telling me right now.

"I don't know" he answers. "But everyone in this situation will ask themselves the same question too" he answers.

He's being serious, isn't he? He's telling the truth, isn't he? So I wasn't going mad when I was turned on, yet felt sick watching Greg and Christina? I am completely sane then?

Feeling a weight lift off my shoulders, as kind Mr Harper guides me downstairs into reception, I can't believe this could all have been avoided, if I had someone to talk to at the time. How was I supposed to know the only person I could have this discussion with was Christina, yet she was going to be the one cheating on me?

"Let me show you something" Mr Harper says, as my deflated body just follows him, heading for the secret passage, probably for the final time.

I haven't got a clue what he wants to show me, but I guess it's going to be reassuring or educational, so why not. He first picks up a sheet covering some computer equipment.

"The control pads" he points out, claiming they've been here all the time.

Next he shows me the hole in the wall, I know I've personally looked through a million times before.

"Look through the hole Jenna" he says.

"Why?" I ask, not liking this bit at all.

"Okay, forget that, come with me instead" he responds, realizing I never want to look through another hole for as long as I live.

We then sit down out in the reception area, where he pulls out his phone.

"Look at this instead" he instructs me.

I look at his phone as requested and there on his screen is the hole we were just standing at. He then flicks the page and shows me the upstairs passage too. Then he goes one better and shows me into the rooms as well.

"You're not the only one that likes to watch, Jenna" he tells me.

Although I should be worried by this, I'm not fazed at all. In-fact, it answers the question of how he knew I killed all these people, doesn't it?

"So you've been watching me all this time, have you?" I ask, not sure whether I believe it or not just yet.

"You're masturbating sessions in the secret passages. The sex you were having in the rooms. Even the games you played with the dead bodies in the basement" he confirms.

Okay, that's a bit freaky, but I can hardly tell him off, when I've pretty much been the star of his show.

"But how?" I ask, confused by something bothering me.

"How what?" he responds, glad I'm taking all these confessions in my stride.

"How did you see everything, if you went home to your wife every night?" I ask, knowing there was something bugging me and this was it.

Once he's confirmed that he didn't watch all the time, but had someone else watching twenty-four hours a day, it all starts to make perfect sense.

"So this other person watched constantly, then edited the highlights for you?" I guess, as he nods, so I ask who.

"Mr Hodge" he responds.

Mr Hodge? Why didn't I guess this straight away? Err, maybe because he just tried to kill me upstairs?

"So was him attacking me earlier a part of your plan too?" I instantly ask, realizing I'm crazy for asking it the minute it leaves my lips.

"No, I didn't know he was going to do that" he answers. "I just paid him to watch all my monitors all the time" he adds.

I don't know what Mr Harper was expecting from me, but I guess it was slightly more than me being so relaxed about his revelations. I guess I've just been through too much to care right now and the information that all women have the possibility of feeling the turn on, hurt thing that I did with Greg has certainly lifted me a lot. To tell the truth, I think he could tell me anything right now and it wouldn't matter, because I'm just so pleased to be sane and alive right now.

"So what happens now then?" I ask, hoping he has a plan for the future now, which hopefully doesn't involve the police.

"We can either frame Mr Hodge for all the murders and keep this place going. Or we can burn it down, run away with your bag full of money and start out somewhere new" he tells me.

Although I like both ideas that don't involve me going to prison or dying, I wasn't actually planning on a future in Mr Harper's company.

"What are you thinking Jenna?" he asks. "Burn the place down, set up a new hotel somewhere else, with more cameras for us to enjoy?" he suggests.

Wow, he's certainly planning a future with me, isn't he?

"I don't know Mr Harper" I respond, before excusing myself to go the bathroom, then maybe clean myself up a bit first.

7:50pm (Saturday 3rd April)

One thing I know for sure as I stand here in this bathroom is, I can't stay here. Every room in this hotel looks the same, so far too many memories are going to haunt me working here now. Maybe we should burn it down and go away. Saying that, why can't we frame Mr Hodge, then go away as a third option?

"Jenna, are you okay in there?" I hear Mr Harper call, whilst I'm locked away in the bathroom, splashing cold water over my face.

"Just a second" I call out, wiping my face dry with a towel, picking up my fuel soaked blouse and covering myself with it, before unlocking the door.

As I walk into the bedroom to give him my final decision, I still don't know which one is.

"HOLY SHIT, MR HARPER. What are you doing?" I leap out of my skin, finding him sitting on the edge of the bed, completely naked.

"Me and you Jenna, setting up together. Me and you and our fascination for watching. Me and you, getting it on right now" he sings out, with a huge smile on his face; which incidentally is the only thing huge in this room right now.

Oh great and he's getting up now. Come on then, walk over towards me, with that thing flapping between your legs. Give me your hottest chat up line, to see if you can get me out of my knickers.

As he stands in front of me, realizing I haven't freaked out about the sex we're about to have, he wraps his arms around me. Holding my blouse in one hand, I drape it over his shoulder, then relax whilst he sinks his teeth passionately into my neck.

"For someone that's been watching me a lot, Mr Harper" I whisper in his ear, biting gently on his lobe. "You don't fucking listen much, do you?"

With that I take the lighter I've been holding since Mr Hodge dropped it upstairs and strike it against my gas soaked blouse. It ignites within seconds and sets fire to his body immediately.

"Why do you think I wanted to have a wash?" I scream at his burning body. "Because I knew you were too good to be true. I knew you'd be a cheat as well. I hate fucking cheats!" I growl at him, claiming the burning of the hotel is my final choice, but only if he burns with it.

Suddenly my little plan backfires literally, as he staggers over towards the door ablaze, trapping me inside the room with him.

"If I'm going to die, so are you" he screams in pain, waving his arms around so I can't escape.

8:30pm (Tuesday 3rd July) – (Three months later)

Well here I am, manageress of my own hotel here in Florida. How did I get out of that room? I was rescued by the police bursting in. How did I get away with the murders I committed? Once I showed the police all the hidden cameras around the hotel and they raided Mr

Hodge's house too, the whole mystery become an open and shut case really. And where did I get the money to buy another hotel, if Mr Hodge had all the money with him at the Cure? Let's just say, although they thought they were clever watching me, they didn't know I was watching them, watch me, so hiding money in a locker on the way back to the hotel, seemed my only clear option that day.

"Welcome to the Cure Hotel, Florida. How can I help you?" I say, welcoming a couple to the desk, in my brand-new establishment, on my first day open to the public. "And are you married, engaged or dating?" I ask next, adding something I plan to quiz every guest about, that visits my hotel from now on.

Be careful who you cheat on visitors,
or you might just find I have the CURE for you too!

(THE STATIC HOUSE DEAL)

Ashley, her agent and the team are continuously checking who is doing what on social media, so would like to thank everyone getting involved in her writing. As a special thank-you, we'd like to offer you something back. So for those of you getting involved, we're offering **bloggers**, **reviewers**, **readers** and **fans** the chance to win every single Ashley book released for **FREE**.

"THAT'S EVERY BOOK FROM THE TIME YOU FIND OUT ABOUT THIS OFFER"

Obviously, we can't give away millions of books, so we've set up an easy enough challenge for you to complete first...

1/ Take a picture of yourself, holding one of Ashley's books.

2/ Write a review on a leading book selling website for Ashley's book, whether it's a masterpiece, just a few lines, or a simple rating.

3/ Rate or review one of Ashley's books on Goodreads and hit that follow button on her page.

4/ Share your picture or the cover of an Ashley book on Facebook / Instagram.

Once you've achieved all four challenges, send your picture to us at: **statichouse@btinternet.com** with the subject of the email titled "***Done***".

Once your claim is verified, you will be awarded a pass, that will allow you Ashley books absolutely FREE for life.

"*No catch*, *no drama*, *no terms and conditions*"

If You do something for Ashley – Ashley wants to do something for you.

Static House Publishing

THE NEXT ASHLEY BOOK DUE TO BE RELEASED

(Tormented By His Soul)

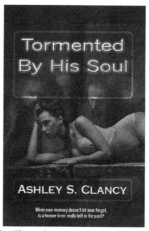

"A chilling thriller about a woman, her ex and how escaping her past isn't as straight forward as it seems"

Printed by Amazon Italia Logistica S.r.l.
Torrazza Piemonte (TO), Italy

11420410R00149